Sarah mounted Gracie and rode along the creek bank behind Uncle Ethan until the waters grew shallow enough to travel up the creek bed. Her heart quickened as she recognized the bend ahead. She urged Gracie up the bank, her thoughts going back to that first day they had seen the meadow beyond it, back before Stoney Creek even had a name.

There was their meadow, surrounded by a semicircle of trees and filled with wildflowers. And over there, on that rise, was the cab . . .

Sarah sucked in her breath. Where the two-room cabin had stood was a black, gaping hole surrounded by a few scattered chimney stones. To one side, the scorched twigs of Ma's peach and apple trees struggled feebly to put on new green leaves.

Everything they had built—the barn, the corn crib, the animal pens—might never have been. Only those horrible ash-covered holes and some scattered poles that once had fenced them in from the wilderness remained to give a hint that the Hiram Moore family had ever settled there. Sarah felt tears sting her eyes and turned helplessly to Uncle Ethan as he rode up beside her.

"Where are they, Uncle Ethan?" Sarah choked out. "Where is my family?"

Be sure to read all the books
in Sarah's Journey

Home on Stoney Creek
Stranger in Williamsburg
Reunion in Kentucky

Also Available as an Audio Book:
Home on Stoney Creek

SARAH'S JOURNEY

REUNION
IN KENTUCKY

Wanda Luttrell

Chariot Books™
A Division of Cook
Communications Ministries

Thanks to Sue Reck, my editor, for her help along this journey.

Chariot Books™ is an imprint of Chariot Family Publishing
Cook Communications, Colorado Springs, CO 80918
Cook Communications, Paris, Ontario
Kingsway Communications, Eastbourne, England

REUNION IN KENTUCKY
© 1995 by Wanda Luttrell

Cover design by Mary Schluchter
Cover illustration by Bill Farnsworth
Interior illustrations by John Zielinski

First printing, 1995
Printed in the United States of America
00 99 98 97 96   5 4 3

Library of Congress Cataloging-in-Publication Data
Luttrell, Wanda.
Reunion in Kentucky/Wanda Luttrell.
p.   cm.
Sequel to: Stranger in Williamsburg.
Summary: Hearing that her mother and new baby sister are seriously ill, thirteen-year-old Sarah leaves her Williamsburg relatives and travels to rejoin her family in the dangerous Kentucky wilderness.
ISBN 0-7814-0907-1
[1. Frontier and pioneer life—Kentucky—Fiction. 2. Kentucky—Fiction. 3. Christian life—Fiction.] I. Title
PZ7.L97954Re   1994
[Fic]--dc20   94-31114
                                                                 CIP
                                                                  AC

Contents

For my son,
John Bradley Luttrell,
who makes my journey through life
an adventure.

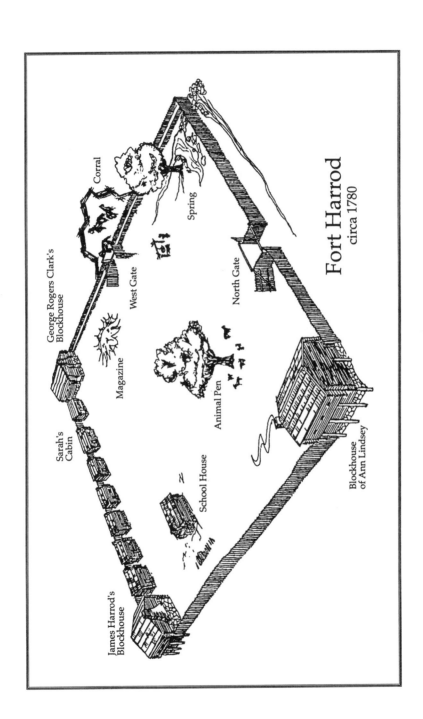

Corral

George Rogers Clark's Blockhouse

West Gate

Spring

Magazine

Sarah's Cabin

Animal Pen

North Gate

School House

James Harrod's Blockhouse

Blockhouse of Ann Lindsey

Fort Harrod
circa 1780

Disappointed that there was no letter for her at the post office again, Sarah Moore walked slowly down Duke of Gloucester Street. The soft June breeze carried the sweet scent of roses and lemon verbena from the fenced gardens of Williamsburg, but she didn't notice.

Sarah was worried about Ma. The new baby should be here by now, but she had heard nothing since Colonel George Rogers Clark had delivered Ma's last letter in December. He had come to Virginia's capital city seeking protection from the Indians for the western settlers who had been under almost constant attack.

As Sarah paused in front of John Greenhow's store, Mrs. Greenhow came running out, waving a folded paper at her. "Here's a letter for you, Sarah!" she called. "It was left by a family coming back east from the settlements just yesterday!"

Sarah took the letter, thanked Mrs. Greenhow, and

stood staring at the red wax that sealed it. She turned the letter over and studied her name on the front of it, savoring the delightful anticipation of reading Ma's news. Then she realized with a shock that the handwriting was not Ma's beautiful, flowing script! The letters were as crooked and squiggly as her own.

Reluctant now to learn what the letter might contain, she unfolded it slowly and read the signature at the bottom. It was signed, "Your brother, Luke." Quickly, she scanned the message:

Sarah, this is to tell you that Ma is very sick. She can't seem to get over the baby's birth. And no wonder! She was born in the woods in a cold February rain, as we fled to the fort from another Indian attack. Daniel Boone and 27 men making salt at Blue Licks were captured.

The doctor here at Harrodstown has bled Ma twice, but she just seems to grow weaker. The baby's not doing well either. Ma thinks she won't live. Betsy and her ma are trying to help, but Mr. Larkin was wounded and requires a lot of care right now. If you could come, Sarah, Ma really needs you.

We are still at the fort, but will likely be back on Stoney Creek by the time you get this. Come as quickly as you can.

Your brother, Luke

Numbly, Sarah folded the letter and put it in her apron pocket. Her thoughts whirled dizzily. Ma was ill! And the baby might die! She took the letter out of her pocket and read it again. Then she began to run toward Nicholson Street.

"There you are, Sarah!" Aunt Charity exclaimed when she burst into the parlor. "We were about to go in to supper without you."

★ Chapter One ★

Silently, Sarah handed Luke's letter to her aunt, who read it, then came to put an arm around her. "Ethan, I have to go to Kentucky," she said, holding the letter out to her husband.

A troubled look came into Uncle Ethan's warm brown eyes as he read the letter. "Charity, you have no idea what you're saying," he said, handing the letter back. "It's not like taking the stagecoach to Richmond! Why, if you survived the journey, you wouldn't know how to cope with the primitive living conditions out there!"

"My sister needs me, Ethan," Aunt Charity insisted. She handed the letter to Tabitha, who carried it over to the harpsichord to share with Abigail. "I could learn to cope with the living conditions," Aunt Charity went on. "Della has."

"And Della apparently is very ill, at least partly due to those conditions. No, Charity, I won't have it!" he said firmly. "I am planning to go to Kentucky with Colonel Clark to do some . . . work for our cause. If Della is able, I will bring her back with me."

"And the baby?" Tabitha asked eagerly as she returned the letter to Sarah.

As he nodded agreement, Megan jumped up and down and clapped her hands. "A baby! I've never had a real baby before!" she exclaimed. "Only my doll and my kitten."

Abigail threw her little sister a withering look. "For pity's sake, Megan, calm down!" she ordered. "We might as well have a squalling baby in the house as you!" She gave Sarah a look that plainly said, "First, I have to share my home with you, and now I'm expected to take in your baby sister as well."

11

★ Reunion in Kentucky ★

I have a little sister! Sarah realized for the first time. *Will she look like me, with straight dark hair and green "cat's eyes," as Luke calls them?* Sarah wished her brother had given more details.

Luke had said, though, that the baby wasn't doing well. He said Ma didn't think she would live. Sarah didn't want her baby sister to die! She didn't even know her name! She wished Luke had . . .

Suddenly, a new and terrible thought hit her. What if Luke had meant that Ma herself was about to die? All at once, she remembered the day she had looked up to see painted Indians in their yard, one of them holding Ma by the hair with his tomahawk raised to scalp her. If he hadn't seen that necklace their Indian friend, the Little Captain, had given Ma, she shuddered to think what might have happened.

Sarah couldn't bear the thought of losing Ma! "I have to go, Uncle Ethan," she said. A sob choked off her words, and she felt Aunt Charity's arms around her again.

"Sarah," her uncle said finally, "I promise I will try to bring Della and the baby back with me—the whole family, if they will come. But I'm sure in the present situation that your ma and pa would not want you back in Kentucky."

"But Ma needs me, Uncle Ethan!" she cried. "I've lived there before. I know the conditions."

"You haven't lived under the conditions they have had lately," he argued. "There's been one Indian raid after another this past year, and the settlers have had to crowd into the forts much of the time. They've had as many as 200 people at Harrodstown, Colonel Clark says, all living in seven small cabins and three blockhouses."

Sarah felt her aunt shudder. "Sarah," she said, "I'm sure

Della has been relieved that you are here safe with us. She said as much in her last letter. She wouldn't want . . ."

"Ma needs me, Aunt Charity!" Sarah repeated desperately.

Her uncle sighed. "I will talk with Colonel Clark, and we will see," he promised vaguely, heading for the dining room.

"I'm sure it will all work out, Sarah," Aunt Charity comforted. "We will pray for your mother and the new little one, and God will provide. Perhaps Ethan will be able to bring them all back to Williamsburg. Won't it be grand having them here with us?"

Tabitha smiled and nodded. Megan, again, clapped her hands. Abigail flounced out of the room.

Don't worry, Abigail, Sarah thought, *they won't come.* She was sure of it. She had to find a way to go to them.

"I'm not hungry, Aunt Charity," Sarah said. "May I be excused from supper?"

Her aunt patted her arm. "Of course, dear," she said with unusual understanding. "I'll have Hester save you something."

Sarah left the house and walked quickly down toward the Governor's Palace to share her news with her friend Marcus. Ever since that day last June when she had discovered him unjustly imprisoned by the cruel stocks and had shared her cold apple juice with him, he had been her special friend.

Passing through the open gates of the tall iron fence enclosing the palace and its grounds, Sarah made her way through the formal sculptured shrubbery near the palace. She followed graveled paths until she found Marcus down near the icehouse, raking leaves off the new green spears of plants in the lower beds.

Marcus was no longer a slave. He had been, until the wife of the king's governor freed him, just before they fled back to England at the start of the Revolution. Now he simply worked as gardener at the palace that housed the governors of the Commonwealth of Virginia.

"What's wrong, Miss Sarah?" Marcus asked, stopping his work after one look at her troubled face. She read Luke's letter to him.

"And you want to go home and be with your mother," he said. He picked up the rake and began to gather the dead leaves into a pile.

Sarah nodded. "She needs me, Marcus. But Uncle Ethan and Aunt Charity don't want me to go. They say Ma wouldn't want me back there with the Indian threat so great now."

"If I was your ma, I'd be doing everything in my power to keep you safe in Williamsburg," he agreed.

"But, Marcus, didn't you listen to what Luke wrote? Ma is very ill, and the baby—or both of them—may die! I have to go!" She brushed impatiently at the tears that slipped down her face.

He nodded solemnly. "I understand, Miss Sarah, I really do," he said. He reached into his pocket, pulled out a clean blue handkerchief, and handed it to her. "When my Dulcie and Sam were taken away," he continued, resting on the rake handle, "the only way I could bear it was to give them to the Lord and trust Him to take care of them. If, as the Good Book says, He knows and cares when a tiny sparrow falls to the ground, you know He's watching out for folks."

"I reckon you're right, Marcus," she agreed doubtfully.

He resumed his raking. "Maybe Colonel Armstrong will

14

help you after all," he suggested.

Sarah shook her head. "He won't, Marcus. He just keeps saying he will go get Ma and the baby and bring them back here."

"Well, then, it appears to me your problem is solved, to everybody's satisfaction," he said.

"But Pa won't leave Kentucky!" Sarah cried. "And Ma won't leave Pa. They will never come with Uncle Ethan. Besides, Ma may not be able to make the journey." She looked up at him out of tear-filled eyes. "Oh, Marcus, what can I do?"

He straightened up and stood looking toward the icehouse on the hill above them. "Let ole Marcus ponder on that awhile, Miss Sarah," he answered, picking up the leaf-filled basket and heading for the compost heap at the bottom of the garden.

Frustrated with his answer, Sarah turned and made her way back through the gardens. Then, just before she entered the formal garden, she heard voices.

"Kaskaskia and Vincennes," a man said. "These are the two fountains from which the thousand little streams of Indian rampage and murder flow down into Kentucky. I want to strike at the source, at the very root of this evil."

That must be Colonel George Rogers Clark, Sarah thought, the red-haired, red-bearded frontiersman who had brought her Ma's letter.

"I am sorry the General Assembly gave you so little," Governor Henry said. She had heard his voice often here in the gardens and recognized it easily. "The Revolution has about drained Virginia's resources. But I have appointed you commander of the western forces, with the authority to do whatever is necessary to defend the settlements."

"Thank you, Governor," Clark responded. "I have been able to secure supplies and some recruits, but I still need men. I have a few at the forts who are willing to accompany me, but the Indians seem to have a limitless supply of fighting braves."

Is Pa one of those men waiting to go with Colonel Clark to the Indian villages? Is Luke? Sarah's second oldest brother was nearing seventeen. It was likely that he would go.

"I'd like to take advantage of these late spring flood tides on the Ohio River," Clark continued. "I have boats waiting at Fort Pitt to get us to the interior. Then we will approach the villages on foot through the forest. It is essential . . ."

Without really thinking, Sarah stepped out from behind the shrubbery and onto the graveled path. The two men stared as she curtsied before them.

★ Chapter One ★

"Governor Henry, Colonel Clark . . ." she began boldly, then stopped, at a loss for words. She reached into her pocket and pulled out Luke's letter. Silently, she held it out to them.

The governor read the letter quickly, then handed it to Clark. "What would you have us do, young lady?" he asked seriously.

"Sir, I must get back to Kentucky! And if Colonel Clark is going, and my Uncle Ethan is going with him, couldn't I go along?"

Colonel Clark refolded the letter and handed it to her, his blue eyes twinkling. "Well, I'd say you have the spunk to make the trip. And I have agreed, against my better judgment, to take thirteen families into Kentucky with me. What's one more?"

Governor Henry smiled. "What does your uncle say?" he asked.

Sarah dropped her gaze to her feet. "He and Aunt Charity think I should stay here because of the Indian danger," she admitted. "But perhaps if you asked him, sir, he would change his mind."

The governor raised skeptical eyebrows. "Ethan Armstrong has a mind of his own, my dear, and so does your Aunt Charity. I doubt . . ."

Suddenly Marcus was beside her. "Governor, sir," he said earnestly, "this young lady needs to go to her mother. And ole Marcus knows you'll do everything in your power to help her, just as you've done these many years to help me try to find my family."

Sarah held her breath for the answer.

"I am meeting with Colonel Armstrong this evening," Clark said finally. "I will talk with him about it," he promised.

"By the way, Marcus," the governor said, throwing an arm around his shoulders and leading him toward the palace, "George has a story to share about a slave who was captured by Indians. I think you need to hear it."

Sarah watched the three men disappear through the back entrance of the pink brick building, then she went over and sat down on the bank of the canal to wait.

"We've found a new tootler, Sarah!" Megan cried excitedly from the front stoop as Sarah came up the walk. "She's not pretty like Gabrielle Gordon, but she's come here all the way from Boston, Massashootus, and she knows all about his'try 'n' jography 'n' everything! Ma says pretty soon I can take some lessons, too, just like you and Tabby and 'Gail!"

"Has Colonel Clark been here, Meggie?" Sarah broke in as soon as the little girl paused for breath. The red-haired frontiersman could have been here and gone twice by now! Sarah had spent more time by the canal than she had realized, rereading Luke's letter and then Ma's, though she didn't really need to read Ma's. She knew it by heart, especially the last paragraph. Ma had written:

I pray for you daily, my sweet daughter, and long to hold you in my arms. But I thank God that you are safe there with your

aunt and uncle. Just remember that I love you very much.
Your mother, Della Moore

It was unlike Ma to put her feelings into words that way, and reading them made Sarah long to be with her.

She sighed. She had loved Williamsburg from the first moment she had seen it almost exactly a year ago. Her brother Nate had brought her to Aunt Charity's to study with her cousins, but the brick house on Nicholson Street wasn't home.

Sarah reckoned the log cabin they had built on the banks of Stoney Creek was the nearest thing she'd had to a home since Pa moved them all to Kentucky. At least her family was there—all but her oldest brother, Nathan, who was with the Patriot army somewhere.

"I don't know, Sarah," Megan pouted. "I've been out with Ma interviewing the new tootler. Haven't you heard a word I've said?"

"It's 'tutor,' Meggie, and, yes, I have," Sarah replied. "That's very exciting news. It's just that I need to go back to Kentucky, and George Rogers Clark might be able to help me."

"I don't want you to go back to Kentucky, Sarah!" Megan interrupted. "What good is an old tootler if your best friend won't be sharing her?"

"I don't want to leave you, either, Meggie. But my ma is very sick, and she needs me. You would want to help your ma if she needed you, wouldn't you?" she asked, taking the little girl's hand and leading her into the house.

Megan thought about that for a few moments, then she nodded. "I guess so," she said. "But Ma never needs me. She's got Tabby and 'Gail and mean old Hester Starkey to help her. She always says, 'Don't get in the way, Megan. Go play with your kitten,' or 'Megan, can't you find something to do out from under our feet?' "

Sarah had to laugh at the little girl's apt imitation of Aunt Charity's voice and mannerisms. Then she sobered. "I really need to know if Colonel Clark has been here," she repeated.

"He has been here, Sarah," her uncle said from the doorway of his study down the hall. "And, though I have grave doubts about the wisdom of my action, I have made arrangements for you to go with us," he said. "Get your things ready, Sarah. We leave at dawn for Fort Pitt. From there, we will take flatboats down the Ohio River into Kentucky."

Sarah caught her breath. "Dawn?" she repeated. "Tomorrow?" But there were so many things she needed to do, so many good-byes to be said!

"You do still want to go, don't you?" Uncle Ethan prompted. "If not, you are welcome to stay here. I promise to do my best to persuade Della to come back with me."

"Oh, no, Uncle Ethan!" she said hastily. "I must go! And I thank you for making it possible. You just surprised me, that's all."

His grin warmed his brown eyes. "You didn't expect me to give in so easily, did you?" he asked.

She shook her head. "Is it all right if I go to John Greenhow's to get some things to take to my family?" she asked then. "I still have some of Pa's money, and if I'm going home, I won't need it."

"We will have to travel light, Sarah," he warned.

"I'll remember, Uncle Ethan. And I promise I'll be ready, and I won't get in your way. You won't be sorry you let me go!" she called as she ran upstairs to get her money and a basket to carry her purchases. Then she ran back down the stairs and out the front door.

Sarah stopped where the Armstrongs' brick walk met Nicholson Street. Should she take the shortcut past Bruton Parish Church to Greenhow's, or should she go the long way around and say good-bye to all the places she had grown to love so well? Deciding on the latter, she turned left down Nicholson and walked past the gaol to the corner. There, she turned right onto Waller Street.

Sarah walked slowly past the little brown house with the blue door where she had spent so many happy hours with their beautiful tutor, Gabrielle Gordon. The house still appeared to be empty, and, since the memories it evoked were painful for her, she turned her attention to Christiana Campbell's sprawling white tavern next door.

How long would it be before she would eat dinner at the genteel Raleigh tavern again? How long before she would again see the pink brick, castle-like building that was Virginia's state Capitol?

She turned right beside the Capitol and walked slowly up Duke of Gloucester Street, past the post office, past the genteel Raleigh Tavern where the Patriot leaders often met to discuss the Revolution, past bawdy Chowning's Tavern where Tabitha's chosen, Seth Coler, had worked until he ran away to join the Patriot army.

Her friend Betsy worked at Chowning's, too. She was an indentured servant, working to pay the cost of her passage to America. Sarah wished she could tell Betsy good-bye, but there was no sign of her, and Aunt Charity would have a fit if Sarah went into Chowning's.

She passed the courthouse, where she had met Marcus.

He had stood in the stocks, receiving punishment for nothing more than being a free man.

One year ago I saw Duke of Gloucester Street for the first time, Sarah thought. She had been convinced it must be the most exciting place in the world, and it was still the most exciting place she had been.

Sarah was determined to go to Ma, but she had to admit she would miss life in Virginia's capital city. She would miss the bustle and the busy shops. She would miss Sunday worship at Bruton Parish Church. She would even miss having to dodge the ranks of marching soldiers as the militia drilled to the cadence of fife and drum.

I will especially miss John Greenhow's store, she thought, going inside to shop for gifts to take her family. Uncle Ethan had said they must travel light, and she didn't have much money to spend. Finally, her choices made and stowed in the basket on her arm, she left the store.

Standing in front of Greenhow's, she looked down Duke of Gloucester Street one last time. "Good-bye!" she whispered, wondering if she would ever see it again. Then she hurried down Palace Green to the gardens.

Sarah found Marcus down by the canal, throwing pieces of stale bread to the geese and swans. How she would miss the beautiful gardens and her favorite spot there by the canal. She had spent so many afternoons watching the swans sail majestically up and down the water! It seemed that whenever trouble came her way, she always came to this place—to think, to cry, to work things out, often with Marcus's help.

"Well, missy," he said when he saw her, "I suppose you've come to tell me good-bye."

Her mouth fell open in surprise. "How did you know,

Marcus?" she asked. "I haven't told anybody yet that I'm leaving!"

"You know I asked Colonel Clark to put in a word for you with your uncle," he answered as a wide grin spread across his face. Then his dark eyes grew sober. "Now I need you to return the favor."

"Of course, Marcus!" she said without hesitation, even though she had no idea what his request might be. "You have come to my rescue many times besides today. How could I refuse to help you?"

"Colonel Clark says there's a story at one of the forts about a slave woman and her son who were captured by the Indians as they were coming to settle in Kentucky. Their owners were killed."

"Oh, Marcus," she broke in excitedly, "do you think it could be Dulcie and Samuel? Do you think Colonel Clark could rescue them? Is he going to try?"

"Whoa, there, missy!" he said, holding up one hand to stop her. "We don't even know the woman's name, much less where she came from. She was from the Islands, you know, before she was brought to Virginia," he interrupted his own story. "Did I ever tell you that?"

She nodded. "Yes, and she could sing like a nightingale."

He looked down at the swans sailing on the canal below them. "And she was as graceful as one of those swans out there," he said softly.

"Tell me about Samuel," Sarah asked quietly.

"That boy could put away enough fried chicken to feed a whole family!" Marcus chuckled. "He loved helping his daddy tend the little garden the plantation owner let Dulcie have behind her cabin, too. Every weekend, I would walk the eight miles out there, and Sammy and I would get the hoes and head for that garden. But that boy loved catfish, too, and he'd hoe real good until he found enough worms to go fishing!" Marcus threw his head back and laughed.

Then he sobered. "It's been many long years, Miss Sarah, since I saw my wife and my little boy. I often wonder what the years have done to my Dulcie. And I reckon Sammy would be practically a grown man!" He stood looking off over the canal, lost in thought.

"You didn't have any other children?" Sarah asked. She had never heard him mention any but Samuel.

He shook his head. "I was in my forties when I met and married Dulcie. We buried three little ones before Sammy came along."

"Anyway," he said finally, "if I had half a thought that it was Dulcie and Samuel out there in Kentucky, I'd be on my way right now! But I don't have much hope it's them. I just have to explore every lead."

"I understand, Marcus," she said. "I know how you must feel."

"No, Miss Sarah, you don't," he said, looking her straight in the eye. "Unless you've had your loved ones sold and taken off to only God knows where, so that you nearly go crazy wondering how they're being treated or if they're still alive, you can't possibly know how it feels."

"You're right, Marcus," she agreed quickly, ashamed of her thoughtless statement. "I know how it feels to want to see your family and to wonder, day by day, if they're still alive. But I have no idea how it feels not knowing where they are and how they are being treated by somebody who claims to own them. It must be awful!" she said, shuddering.

"Well, if you could make inquiries for me about these Indian captives, I'd be much obliged," he said. "If you find out her name is Dulcie, let me know, and I'll come running, just in case she's my Dulcie. You can send word by your uncle when he comes back to Williamsburg."

"I will do my best, Marcus," Sarah promised, knowing there was nothing she'd rather do than find Dulcie and Sam for her friend.

Suddenly, she threw her arms around the old man. "Oh, Marcus, I'm going to miss you!" She could feel tears gathering.

As he had done so many times before, he handed her a clean blue handkerchief. "Ole Marcus will miss you, too," he said, patting her on the shoulder. "Take that hand-kerchief with you to remind you of me, missy, and, if the time comes for shedding tears, use it and remember that you have someone back here in Williamsburg who cares."

26

★ Chapter Two ★

Sarah couldn't speak for the lump in her throat, and Marcus went on, "And take my guiding verses from the third chapter of Proverbs to remind you of Him: 'Trust in the Lord with all thine heart; and lean not unto thine own understanding. In all thy ways acknowledge him, and he shall direct thy paths.' "

Sarah studied his smooth face and caring dark eyes, storing up the memory of them for the time when she wouldn't be able to see them.

"You'll be back one of these days," he predicted. "Nobody leaves Williamsburg and never comes back."

She nodded. Then, before the tears could spill over, clutching the handkerchief, she ran from the gardens without looking back.

Sarah walked along the Ohio River in Pittsburgh, watching Colonel Clark as he commanded his men loading the flatboats for the trip down the river into Kentucky.

The would-be settlers he had been persuaded to take along "to add to the able-bodied riflemen in Kentucky," were loading everything they owned onto the flatboats. Sarah wished Ma had been able to take a couple of trunks like this lady here, or a couple of big barrels like that one over there, likely packed with pretty linens and china and books and all sorts of nice things to make their new homes in the wilderness more pleasant. She supposed they would settle somewhere along one of the rivers, since there was no way they could transport so many belongings through the thick forest on horseback.

Pa said Kentucky would have roads, shops, churches, and schools someday. He said someday its crude log cabins would be replaced by brick and frame houses as fine as any in Virginia. But "someday" was a long way off, as far as Sarah could see. She wondered if any of these ladies embarking on this long, dangerous journey into a wild, lonely place really knew just how primitive their new homes would be.

She watched Uncle Ethan load Gracie and Jake onto a boat with other horses. Then he took her deerskin bag in one hand and reached up with the other to help her onto the boat they would share with several families.

"What on earth have you got in this bag, Sarah?" he asked.

"Not much, Uncle Ethan," she answered truthfully, for she had few possessions. Into the bag she had packed Abigail's brown hand-me-down dress, the two new dresses Aunt Charity had made her, the soft red dress Ma had made her for their first Christmas on Stoney Creek, her undergarments, and her nightgown. She had on the homespun dress she had worn when she came to Williamsburg, and she carried her cloak over her arm.

"Well," she added honestly, "I did tuck in a parcel of those little chocolate nonpareils for Luke and Jamie, and a packet of cinnamon and a pretty horn comb for Ma, but none of those weighs much. I reckon the weight is from the square iron nails and the two iron hinges I brought for Pa to replace the squeaky leather ones on our cabin door."

Uncle Ethan laughed. "Well, here's something to add to your collection," he said, handing her the little leather-bound volume of *The Pilgrim's Progress* she had borrowed from his library so often.

"Uncle Ethan!" she exclaimed. "How did you know I liked it? And are you sure you don't want it?"

"Your Aunt Charity told me you were starting to read it

for the third time, so it was pretty obvious you liked it," he answered with a grin. "And it's not that I don't want it, but that I want you to have it. Books surely must be scarce on the frontier."

"Oh, they are, Uncle Ethan. Thank you!" she said.

"You are welcome, Sarah. I will try to see that you get more books another time, when we don't have to travel so light." He turned then to help another family with their loading.

At last, the men untied the ropes holding the boats to the shore, and, one by one, the current caught them and swept them off downstream. Sarah sat down quickly to keep from being thrown overboard as the boats jerked and twisted and whirled, traveling at the mercy of the flooded river.

For several days and nights—Sarah soon lost count—

they continued their erratic journey downstream. The men constantly struggled against the wayward current, against hidden boulders and submerged logs that would cripple the wooden boats. Those not fighting the river were on a constant watch for any Indians who might be lurking in the miles of untamed wilderness which lined the shores.

Then one evening, Colonel Clark ordered the boats ashore a large island in the middle of the river. This would be the settlers' new home. He put them to work fortifying the place against Indian attack and set them to clearing land and planting corn. Before long, weary of his demands, the settlers began to call the place "Corn Island."

Feeling quite anxious to get back to Stoney Creek, Sarah was glad when Colonel Clark decided it was time for the soldiers and their boats to move on down the river. When she heard him give the command to "shoot the falls!" however, she wasn't so sure how glad she was to be there. Instead of unloading the boats and carrying everything around the falls on land, they took the boats straight over the falls—horses, people, and all! Sarah was glad these falls were not as high as the giant waterfall Pa had shown them on the Cumberland River, but it was still a totally terrifying experience.

Miraculously, all the boats landed safely upright below the falls, some of the men praying, some of them swearing, and all of them poling frantically to keep the boats afloat and steer them back into the current.

The journey continued until finally their boat pulled to shore at the mouth of Stoney Creek. Sarah and Uncle Ethan led their horses onto the sandy bank, and the soldiers cheered and waved as they floated on down the river and out of sight around the bend.

★ Chapter Three ★

Sarah mounted Gracie and rode along the creek bank behind Uncle Ethan until the waters grew shallow enough to travel up the creek bed. Her heart quickened as she recognized the bend ahead. She urged Gracie up the bank, her thoughts going back to that first day they had seen the meadow beyond it, back before Stoney Creek even had a name.

There was their meadow, surrounded by a semicircle of trees and filled with wildflowers. And over there, on that rise, was the cab . . .

Sarah sucked in her breath. Where the two-room cabin had stood was a black, gaping hole surrounded by a few scattered chimney stones. To one side, the scorched twigs of Ma's peach and apple trees struggled feebly to put on new green leaves.

Everything they had built—the barn, the corn crib, the animal pens—might never have been. Only those horrible ash-covered holes and some scattered poles that had once fenced them in from the wilderness remained to give a hint that the Hiram Moore family had ever settled there. Sarah felt tears sting her eyes and turned helplessly to Uncle Ethan as he rode up beside her.

"Oh, Sarah, I'm so sorry!" he said huskily, taking in the desolation before them. "Are you positive this is the right place?"

She nodded, fighting tears. She heard the creak of leather as Uncle Ethan dismounted, and watched numbly as he walked over to the spot where the cabin had stood. He stooped to feel the ashes, then stood and looked down toward the creek.

Sarah's gaze followed his to the creek. The mill that ground their corn and wheat was gone. All that remained

33

was the rock wall she, Pa, Ma, and Luke had built at the cost of so many callouses and aching bones. Only the wall and the abandoned mill stones lying in the creek bore silent witness to the fact that a mill had been there.

Where was her family? Were they still at the fort? Or were they all dead, killed by the Indians who had burned their cabin?

"The fire was awhile back," Uncle Ethan said. "Most likely set by Indians. If the cabin had caught fire from a faulty chimney, the other buildings were far enough away to survive. And that scattered fence says it was Indians, aiming to erase every trace of the settlers they hate so!"

"Where are they, Uncle Ethan?" Sarah choked out.

"The Indians? Oh, I'd say they're miles from here now. There's nothing left for them to . . ."

"No, Ma and Pa. And Luke and Jamie. And the new baby. Where are they?" She could hear her voice rising hysterically.

His eyes met hers, then looked away. He busied himself mounting his horse. Finally he cleared his throat. "Well, they could have been warned and gone into one of the forts. Or they could have been . . ."

"Killed!" she broke in, almost in a panic.

He reached over to pat her hand clutching the saddle horn. "It's not likely, Sarah," he said. "There are no . . . remains here. Indians don't bury their victims. So either your folks got away to safety, or . . ."

"Or what, Uncle Ethan?" she begged, reaching into her pocket to get Marcus's blue handkerchief to wipe away the tears slipping down her face and dropping off her chin.

"Or they've been taken captive," he answered softly.

Captive! The ugly word shivered through her like an

34

arrow, her mind recalling the horrible stories she had heard about what Indians did with their captives.

"Were there other settlements here?" Uncle Ethan interrupted her morbid thoughts.

She nodded, pointing upstream. "The Larkins' place was just beyond that next bend, and past them was the Johnson place. But the Johnsons were burned out before I left and went back east."

Uncle Ethan turned his horse in the direction she indicated. Numbly, Sarah turned Gracie and followed, knowing that they would find the Larkin settlement to be simply a repeat of what they had seen there—blackened holes and scattered stones. At the Johnson place, bushes and weeds were already reclaiming the meadow where their buildings had stood.

"We'll ride on to the fort," Uncle Ethan said, taking a paper out of the stained leather pouch he always carried. "Someone there will have word of what happened here. And, most likely, your folks will be there, safe and sound," he added, smiling reassuringly at her as he unfolded the map and began to study it.

Sarah nodded, trying to swallow the lump that had lodged in her throat. She wished she could be as sure as Uncle Ethan about finding her family at Harrodstown.

A day and a half later, Sarah and Uncle Ethan rode across the clearing toward the log stockade. As the first time Sarah had come to the fort, guns appeared along the sharp-pointed logs, aimed right at them.

Sarah remembered how disappointed she had been the first time she entered Harrodstown. She had expected a real town, but it was only a makeshift town with a few poor one-room log cabins huddled behind funny-looking walls. The walls, made by standing sharpened logs on end and fastening them side by side, looked like a row of sharp slate pencils standing on the blunt end.

Sarah's glance fell on the crude stones which marked the graves of settlers beside the stockade. The cemetery had grown considerably since she was there last. Did any of her family lie there among the graves that surely now outnumbered the settlers still living inside Fort Harrod?

"I am Ethan Armstrong from Williamsburg," Uncle Ethan called out. "And this is my niece, Sarah Moore. We seek the Hiram Moore family, settlers on Stoney Creek. Have you news of them?"

The log gates swung slowly open, and Sarah's heart beat faster as they rode inside. Would her family be there?

As the gates swung shut behind them, and the people of Harrodstown crowded around, Uncle Ethan repeated, "Have you news of the Moore family?"

"That we do, sir," a woman answered.

Sarah felt her heart stop, then start again. "Mrs. Larkin?" she cried. "Is it you? Is my? . . . Are they? . . ." She couldn't finish the questions.

"Are the Moores here?" Uncle Ethan finished for her. "We found their cabin and farm buildings burned to the ground."

"Ours, too, I'm sure," Mrs. Larkin replied. "We've all been here since we received warning of Indian attack some months back. Hiram and Luke and my sons have gone to meet Colonel Clark and go on the Indian raids. You just missed them. Your ma is poorly, Sarah," she added, "and that poor little baby just whimpers a pitiful mewing sound like a sickly kitten. Betsy and I have been doing what we can, but . . ." She shook her head. "I wish I had better news."

"And Jamie?" Sarah asked. "Is he? . . ."

"Oh, he's over at our place, playing with Ruthie. Betsy keeps an eye on him most of the time, just like he was her own."

Sarah swallowed a quick thrust of jealousy. She was grateful that Jamie had someone to care for him.

"Come, child. I'll take you to the cabin," Mrs. Larkin said. "Your ma will be glad to lay eyes on you! Maybe it will perk her up some."

"I'll be along to see Della later, Sarah," Uncle Ethan said, handing her the deerskin bag he had taken from behind Gracie's saddle. "I'll be in the Harrod blockhouse here until tomorrow morning. And I'm leaving Gracie here for you, in case you need her."

"Thank you, Uncle Ethan, for everything," Sarah said, giving him a quick hug. She took the bag and followed Mrs. Larkin across the compound to the row of cabins along one wall of the fort. At the second one from the corner, they stopped and Mrs. Larkin pushed open the door.

Sarah stood in the doorway, letting her eyes adjust to the dimness inside. Then she saw a thin, pale figure lying on the rough wooden bed, the covers barely mounded over the slight form under them. Sarah turned to Mrs. Larkin, her eyes filled with questions. Surely they had entered the wrong cabin! This old, worn woman with the dull brown hair could not be her mother!

Suddenly, the woman awoke and stared at them from eyes sunken into dark sockets, hollowed out of a thin, white face. Then the eyes widened. She tried to rise up on one elbow, but fell back weakly. Mrs. Larkin hurried to lift the woman and prop pillows behind her. The sunken eyes never left Sarah's face. "Sarah?" she whispered hoarsely.

Then, as tears began to spill down the pale cheeks, Sarah ran to Ma and clasped her hand, afraid to hug her lest the thin bones break with the pressure.

"Oh, Sarah, I've missed you so!"

Sarah kissed Ma's cheek. "I've missed you, too, Ma!" she choked.

After a few moments, Ma pulled her hand out of Sarah's and pushed back the covers beside her. "See your new baby sister, Sarah? Her name is Elizabeth, and she'd be pretty like you if only she wasn't so thin and sickly. Look, she has your pa's blue eyes," she added as the baby awoke and began the pitiful mewing sound Mrs. Larkin had described.

Mrs. Larkin came quickly and picked up Elizabeth, crooning to her.

Sarah stood there wondering if little Elizabeth would live, if Ma would ever be strong and healthy once more.

Nothing will ever be right for us again! she thought. *I wish we'd never come to this terrible place!*

Lightning flashed, followed by a crack of thunder that shook the cabin. Sarah could hear big drops of rain beginning to fall on the wooden roof shingles.

She glanced over at the corner where Ma lay propped on pillows against the bedstead. "Let me plump those pillows, Ma," she said, going over to the bed. "Maybe this rain will freshen the air. It's so stuffy in here."

Ma smiled up at her weakly. Sarah's heart wrenched as she felt the sharpness of Ma's bones beneath her skin, as she raised her up, then lowered her against the freshened pillows. Ma's face, with the dark circles under her eyes, was as pale as the pillow covers.

Sarah sighed, wishing she knew what to do to help Ma regain her strength. The doctor had gone over to Fort Boonesborough for a while, and there was no one here to tell her what to do.

She crossed back over to the fireplace, took the long-handled wooden ladle from its peg on the mantel, and stirred the soup bubbling in the iron kettle. It was too hot for a fire, but she had needed one to cook supper. The rain, though, was cooling things down a bit.

Sarah dipped up a ladleful of vegetable soup and poured it into a pottery bowl that must have been made by a potter in Harrodstown. She didn't recognize it from their home on Stoney Creek.

Sarah carried the soup over to the bed, glad that Mrs. Larkin had taken the baby to her cabin for the afternoon. It would be all she could do to coax Ma to swallow these few spoonfuls of soup without the baby's pitiful crying to disturb her. When little Elizabeth cried that hopeless, whimpering cry, Ma just lay there with tears seeping out below her eyelids and spilling down her sunken cheeks.

Ma was convinced the baby was going to die, and Sarah was afraid she was right. Elizabeth was so tiny, and Ma had lost the ability to feed her. Mrs. Larkin was trying her on cow's milk, but the little thing just couldn't keep it down. She seemed to be all big hungry eyes as her body grew smaller and smaller.

If she weren't so sickly, little Elizabeth would likely be pretty, with Pa's Irish eyes and Ma's red-gold highlights in her hair, what little there was of it. Would she have curly hair like Ma, as Sarah herself always had wanted? Would she live to grow pert and bubbly like her little cousin, Megan? Would Elizabeth ever be able to follow Sarah around as Megan had done, and as Jamie had done before she left for Williamsburg? Would she ever be strong and healthy like sturdy little Jamie?

Sarah would have to go get Jamie soon. It was good of Betsy to take over his care while Ma was so ill. At four years old, he could be a handful. And Sarah had to admit that Jamie was happier over at the Larkins' cabin playing with Ruthie, who was near his age, and being cared for by Betsy, who apparently had taken his sister's place in his affections.

Sarah recalled the first evening back in Harrodstown, a week ago now, after she had seen Ma and the baby and had gone to the Larkins' to get Jamie. It still hurt to remember how he had stared at her with wide, solemn eyes, then edged over to stand close to Betsy, holding tightly to her skirt with one chubby little hand.

Betsy had tried to coax him. "It's Sarah, Jamie. Don't you remember your big sister? He missed you terribly at first," she apologized to Sarah.

Jamie, though, had just stared at her solemnly, the fingers of one hand going into his mouth, the other still clinging to Betsy's skirt. When Sarah tried to pry him loose to take him home with her, he had thrown both arms around Betsy and cried as though his little heart would break.

Finally, Mrs. Larkin had persuaded Sarah to let him stay with them. "Just till he gets used to you again," she said. "You don't want him disturbing your ma and the baby," she reminded her, and reluctantly, Sarah had agreed.

If she had had more time, she might have tried harder to win back Jamie's affections right away. But her time was filled with taking care of Ma and the baby, and she patiently spooned more hot soup into Ma's mouth and waited for her to swallow. Then she quickly offered another spoonful, trying to get all the nourishment down Ma she could, before Ma began to shake her head and refuse it.

If only there were somebody around here who knew what to do for Ma and the baby! Sarah thought desperately. She wished

Aunt Charity were there, or even the sour old housekeeper, Hester Starkey. Together, they knew how to deal with just about anything!

Sarah closed her eyes, remembering her aunt's beautiful home in Williamsburg—the polished tables and chests, the dainty china, the soft carpets, the clean scent of wax and polish, the pleasant odor of lemon and bayberry soaps and candles, the fresh breeze blowing through lacy curtains at open windows.

She opened her eyes and looked around her. She knew Pa had been lucky to be able to buy this tiny log cabin and its contents from that family going back east last summer. And, while the little one-room structure was poor compared to her aunt and uncle's home in Williamsburg, it was as good as most here in the fort.

Their cabin on Stoney Creek had been nicer, though, and they'd had a lot more room. Sarah wondered if Pa would ever rebuild. Maybe all this trouble would convince him to take them back to Virginia when he and Luke returned from the Indian raids. Last spring, when she and Nathan had traveled by their old place at Miller's Forks on their way to Williamsburg, they had found the farm deserted and the buildings showing signs of neglect. Maybe Pa could buy it back, and they could all settle down there again and be happy.

Then the thought came to her that Ma was not able to travel back to Virginia, or anywhere else. She was too weak to walk across the cabin floor, much less make such a hard journey! So they were stuck there, at least for a while, and she supposed she might as well make the best of it. She certainly couldn't go back and leave Ma in the condition she was in.

★ **Chapter Four** ★

Sarah couldn't get on with her plans to find Dulcie and Samuel, either. Not now. But as soon as Ma was stronger, she promised herself, she would find out if the slave woman who had been captured by the Indians was Dulcie. If so, she would get her back. Somehow.

"I'm so glad to have you with me, Sarah," Ma breathed. Then the tears welled up in her eyes and spilled down her sunken cheeks.

"Oh, Ma, please don't start crying again," Sarah begged, wiping futilely at the flood that couldn't be stopped once it had begun.

"Life here is so hard, Sarah, and with me so no account . . ."

"Hush, Ma!" Sarah begged, feeling her own tears gathering. "I would never have forgiven Luke if he hadn't let me know how sick you were! And I want to be here with you as long as you need me."

"It's so hard here!" Ma repeated weakly.

"Do you regret it, Ma?" Sarah blurted before she thought. "Do you regret coming to Kentucky?"

Pain migrated across Ma's face and settled in her eyes. "In some ways, I do," she answered softly. "But the childbirth fever could have hit me in Virginia just as well, I reckon. I just wish you had never come back, Sarah. For your sake!" she choked. "You'll be an old, broken woman before your life really begins." The tears rolled down her cheeks again.

Sarah knew she had to change the subject. She should never have brought it up. "Ma, don't cry," she begged. "Things will seem better when you gain your strength back, and when Pa and Luke return from the Indian raids."

Ma shook her head. "This place is a killer, Sarah. It's killed all our hopes and dreams, and it's about killed me.

Who knows if your pa and Luke will survive this escapade of Clark's, and I know little Elizabeth is going to die."

"Hush!" Sarah repeated. "Don't say such things! We'll . . ."

Ma grabbed her arm with one bony hand. Her grasp was surprisingly strong for her weakened condition. "Promise me, Sarah!" she urged, shaking her arm in agitation.

Sarah bent to hear the whispered words. "What, Ma? What is it you want?"

"Promise me you'll get out of here as soon as I'm gone. If the baby lives, take her to your Aunt Charity. But no matter what, promise me you will go back to Williamsburg. I was wrong to bring all of you out here. But your pa was so set on it. And now, no doubt he and Luke are lying dead out there in the forest."

"Please, Ma," Sarah begged, "don't carry on so! You'll make the fever come back. Please calm down. Let me get you a cold drink of water and some of those powders the doctor left. You need to rest while Mrs. Larkin is watching the baby for us."

Gently, she removed Ma's fingers from her arm, picked up the empty soup bowl, and went to the water bucket. She plunged the gourd dipper into the bucket, hearing it scrape bottom as she dipped up half a cup of water and poured it into a clean cup. She shook a dose of the doctor's powders into it.

"The water isn't fresh, Ma," she apologized as she lifted her so she could drink. "I'll go to the spring and bring you a good, cold drink as soon as I can, but I think you should have this now."

Ma drained the cup and sank back against the pillows. She looked up at Sarah with sad, dark eyes. "I'm so sorry, little girl!" she whispered, the tears gathering again.

★ **Chapter Four** ★

"Ma, please!" Sarah begged. "If you care about me, about all of us, try to rest and gain some strength. I'm sure Pa and Luke are fine. Uncle Ethan says Colonel Clark is a brilliant military leader. . . ."

"Pray for them, Sarah!" Ma urged. "And for Nate. Pray hard!"

"I will, Ma," she promised. "Now, rest. I'll be right here when you wake up, and we can talk then." She patted Ma's hand gently.

Sarah sat by the bed for a while, praying silently for Pa and Luke, for Nate, for Ma and the baby. But she wondered if God really heard her prayers. Sometimes the things she prayed for happened, she admitted, but was it all coincidence? Just as often, her prayers seemed to float off into the sky without any evidence that God heard.

She sighed, got up to carry the cup over to the table, and set it beside the soup bowl to be washed later. She threw a glance back at the bed. Ma seemed to be sleeping. The powders had done their work. She would likely rest now for an hour or two, but the powders did nothing to strengthen her. They simply put her to sleep.

Sarah threw a shawl over her head and shoulders and reached for the water bucket. She'd better get that fresh water while she had the chance, rain or no rain. At least the thunder and lightning had stopped, she noticed gratefully as she pulled the door to behind her.

To avoid the mud, Sarah didn't take her usual shortcut diagonally across the compound to the spring. She followed the path in front of their cabin and the one next door, stepping on stones the settlers had placed before their homes.

When she looked up, she was staring straight through

45

the open doorway of the big corner blockhouse that belonged to Colonel George Rogers Clark and into the face of a woman as dark as Marcus. The woman sat on the bottom step of the stairway that led to the second story of this taller cabin, crooning some wordless melody to the chubby little white baby in her arms.

Elizabeth had cried all day yesterday, and Ma's fever had been up, so Sarah hadn't been able to watch much of the family's moving into the nearby cabin. Did the newcomers from Boonesborough have slaves, or was this a hired servant? Ben Logan's family over at Saint Asaph had four slaves, and she had heard there were some on settlements scattered across Kentucky, but she had not seen any in Harrodstown. She didn't know if there were any at Boonesborough.

"Can I help you, missy?" the woman asked

"I'm sorry!" Sarah stammered. "I didn't mean to stare. It's just that . . ." Suddenly a wild thought struck Sarah. "Pardon me, ma'am, but your name's not Dulcie, is it?"

The woman studied her out of dark, unreadable eyes. Finally, she shook her head slowly from side to side. "No, missy. My name be Malinda," she said, "and I be from Barbados. By way of South Carolina. Both of which be soft and fair and safe." She rolled her eyes in the direction of the big room on Sarah's right, where Sarah glimpsed a pretty blonde woman reading to three little girls.

Malinda lowered her voice, but only slightly. "Anybody gotta be head-touched to leave either one of them for a terrible place like this!" she muttered.

Sarah laughed.

"Malinda!" the woman scolded gently. Then she looked at the sleeping baby in Malinda's arms. "I declare, that

46

baby's been asleep for half an hour," she said, closing her book and standing up. "You may lay him on the bed now and come help with supper."

Malinda rolled her eyes again, this time in Sarah's direction, and heaved her large body up from the step. When Sarah looked back, she was taking her own sweet time about carrying the baby to the bed.

Sarah went on her way to the spring, wondering about this latest family that Colonel Clark had let move into one room of his blockhouse. She had heard Mrs. Larkin say the woman's husband had been killed by Indians a few weeks ago. What had she said their name was—Richards? No, Reynolds. That was it. When she had more time, Sarah thought, she would like to get to know them.

On her way back from the spring, Sarah found the door to the blockhouse closed.

$\mathbf{M}$a's fever was back up, and she was begging for a cold drink of water, so Sarah was, again, on her way to the spring. This time, to keep little Elizabeth's weak cries from distressing Ma, Sarah had taken her along. She carried the baby in her left arm and the empty wooden bucket in her right.

Malinda was just ahead of her, swinging her own empty bucket in one hand. "That be your baby?" she asked as she dipped her bucket of water from the bubbling spring. Then she offered, "Let me hold the little thing while you get your water."

Gratefully, Sarah handed her the baby. "She's my baby sister, Elizabeth," she explained. "Ma's been sick ever since she was born."

"Oh, missy!" Malinda exclaimed. "This poor little bag of bones be not long for this world unless something soon changes!"

Sarah turned quickly to dip up water, not wanting to hear the dreadful words that only bore out what Ma had been saying all along.

"This be a harsh land," Malinda went on, "and many babies, as well as older folks, will be planted in its soil before it is settled, I fear. What's wrong with this little one?"

Suddenly the words tumbled out of Sarah's mouth—all the pent-up worry and distress over Ma and the baby, all her unanswered prayers, all the loneliness and fear and hopelessness.

"There, now, missy," Malinda soothed, wiping Sarah's tears away with the corner of her apron. "Mistress Anabelle Reynolds be a kindhearted lady. She likely to let Malinda come after chores to lend you a hand. You run on home now, and after 'while we'll see what we can do for this little one. And for your ma, too. Malinda be knowing a trick or two."

Sarah tucked the baby back over her left hip, and reached for the heavy bucket, suddenly aware of how tired she was.

"Let Malinda carry that for you as far as she goes," the woman said, taking the bucket and letting it balance the one she already carried in her other hand.

Sarah followed, cuddling Elizabeth's thin body against her own. *She's not much heavier than that rag doll I carried all the way to Kentucky two years ago,* Sarah thought. "Poor little sister," she whispered. "I wish you could be strong. I wish you could let out a loud, healthy cry instead of this pitiful little mewing sound."

Back in the cabin, Sarah held Ma's head so she could sip from the cold water in the cup. Then she bathed the baby and dressed her in clean, dry clothes.

Sarah supposed it wouldn't hurt to let Malinda try to help them. As she bathed Ma's hot forehead and hands with cold water, she admitted that neither Ma nor Elizabeth was getting better this way. She just didn't know what to do for them!

True to her word, Malinda showed up right after supper, and she wasted no time spooning some hot liquid into Ma and resettling her in the bed. Ma smiled sleepily, and in no time had drifted off to sleep. When Sarah next went to check on her, Ma's fever had broken and perspiration was curling thin tendrils of hair around her face. With her eyelids hiding the darkness that had settled in her eyes, and with a peaceful look on her sleeping face, Ma showed traces of the pretty woman she had been.

Malinda was busily stirring some thick liquid over the fire. She poured a little milk into it, and set it on the table.

Then she picked up Elizabeth, sat down on one of the benches with her in one arm, and began to put the mixture into her little mouth with the tip of one finger. Elizabeth strangled a little, then began to suck hungrily at Malinda's finger.

"This chile be hungry," Malinda crooned as she dipped up more liquid and carried it to the baby's mouth. "That's all that's wrong with this little one!" Before long, the mixture was all inside Elizabeth, and Malinda was holding her over her shoulder, patting her expertly on the back. Instead of whimpering, Elizabeth was nodding contentedly against the big woman. Soon she was asleep, and Malinda laid her in a nest of covers in the trundle bed.

"Malinda be back in the morning, early, before chores begin," she whispered as she left the cabin.

"Good night," Sarah whispered back, "and thank you!"

Malinda waved one hand to dismiss the need for thanks as she plodded down the path toward the blockhouse.

Walking on tiptoe, Sarah undressed and put on her nightgown. She crawled carefully into bed beside the sleeping baby, dreading the time when Elizabeth would wake up, whimpering.

When Sarah awoke, she was amazed to see that a faint light was showing around the window shutter. Both Ma and Elizabeth were still sleeping.

She heard something near the fireplace, and was surprised to see that Malinda was there, stirring something over a blazing fire. Sarah hadn't even heard her come into the cabin!

Sarah sighed and sank back onto the pillow. Just knowing Malinda was there seemed to lift a load from her shoulders. At least someone was trying to help Ma and the baby, someone who surely knew more about it than she did.

When Sarah awoke the second time, Malinda was gone. Elizabeth was lying on her back, contentedly cooing to herself as she examined her tiny fingers.

Ma smiled at Sarah weakly from against her pillows. Sarah saw that she was wearing a clean white gown trimmed with pink roses, and there was a pink ribbon holding back her hair.

"Where on earth did you find that woman, Sarah?" she asked. "She's surely a miracle sent from God!"

Sarah smiled back, wondering if Ma were right, if Malinda was the answer to her desperate prayers.

The baby lay quietly all morning. When she did begin to fret, Sarah fed her some of the mixture Malinda had left, and she took a long peaceful nap.

Ma rested better that day than she had since Sarah had been there. She had no fever, and she even ate a little of the fresh baked bread and mutton stew Mrs. Larkin brought over at noontime.

After lunch, Ma asked for the Bible, but she was too weak to hold up the heavy book to read in bed. Sighing, she laid it beside her.

"Do you want me to read to you, Ma?" Sarah offered.

"Yes, please," Ma said, pushing the Bible toward her. "Read the Ninety-first Psalm, about how the arrow that flies by day and the pestilence that stalks by night shall not come near us."

Sarah swallowed hard, then began to read, knowing Ma was worried about Luke and Pa, and Nate, and Elizabeth and herself—about all the things over which they had no control. She remembered Ma reading that psalm to them when Pa was gone and they were alone in the cabin on Stoney Creek. ". . . Because he hath set his love upon me, therefore will I deliver him: I will set him on high, because he hath known my name. He shall call upon me, and I will answer him: I will be with him in trouble; I will deliver him, and honour him. With long life will I satisfy him, and shew him my salvation," she finished.

Was knowing God's name like acknowledging Him, as Marcus's favorite verse said? Sarah supposed that meant letting people know you believed in Him, but almost everybody believed in God! And a lot of people said things like, "Praise the Lord!" when good things happened or "God help us!" when they didn't. Was that what was meant by acknowledging Him?

She wished Marcus were there so she could ask him about it. He was sure to have an explanation, and probably some story to make it clear.

Sarah glanced at Ma, and seeing that she had drifted off to sleep, closed the Bible and laid it on the mantel.

She slipped out to visit Jamie again at the Larkins, but except for a brief "H'lo," at Betsy's urging, he totally ignored her.

What can I do to win him back? Sarah agonized as she returned to the cabin to check on Ma and the baby. They were both still sleeping, so she took a basket to the garden to gather greens for supper. Jamie had put her completely out of his life, and his indifference really hurt. *If only Malinda could prepare a mixture that would put love back in Jamie's heart for me!* she thought. But not even Malinda could do that.

That evening, Malinda was back, cheerfully ministering to Ma and the baby while Sarah finished preparations

54

for a meal of greens and corn bread.

"You truly are a miracle, Malinda!" she said admiringly, as she watched the woman coax Ma into eating a whole bowl of some mixture she had brought with her. She then fed little Elizabeth with a "bottle" she had made from an animal membrane.

"God sometimes be working in mysterious ways, missy, and if He see fit to use Malinda for one of His miracles, why not?" she answered, preparing to leave.

"Can you stay and eat with me?" Sarah asked, eager for someone to talk with as she ate the meal she had fixed. Maybe Malinda could explain to her about acknowledging God.

Again, Malinda studied her out of those unreadable dark eyes. "All right, missy, and I thank you kindly," she agreed finally, taking a seat on one of the benches as Sarah dished up the food.

Sarah soon found that Malinda didn't make conversation while she ate, though. She concentrated entirely on eating the food and drinking the milk Sarah set before her, getting up once to help herself to more greens and corn bread.

The meal reminded Sarah of an evening she had eaten this same fare at Marcus's table. She had begged him to help her contact Gabrielle before the Patriots deported her for her spying activities on behalf of the British.

Sarah missed Marcus. She wished she could do something really special for him. He had been such a good friend to her when she was a lonely stranger in Williamsburg. If only she could find his wife and son and reunite them after all his years of fruitless searching! Marcus had been told that the slave trader who bought them said he was heading for Kentucky. But even if the man had lied, as Marcus suspected, and had taken them south to the cotton plantations instead, South Carolina was south and grew cotton.

"Malinda, did you ever know a slave woman named Dulcie?" Sarah asked as the woman sopped up the last of the juice on her plate with the last piece of corn bread. She knew it was unlikely. *But miracles do happen*, she thought. *Malinda wouldn't be here if they didn't!*

Silently, Malinda studied her empty plate as though the answer were written there.

"She was slender and pretty, I am told," Sarah went on, "and she could sing like a nightingale, though I don't know if she ever sang again after they took her and her little boy away from her husband."

Malinda stood up, walked over to the fireplace, and stood staring into the dying embers. She sighed deeply and turned to face Sarah.

"There be talk over at Boonesborough of a black woman and her chile who were captured by the Indians. They belonged to a family from down south somewhere who were coming to settle in Kentucky. Only God knows why!" she interjected. "The family was killed and scalped as they camped by the trail one night. One slave escaped and made his way to the fort to tell the story."

"And did they ever find the woman and her child?" Sarah asked, excited by the possibility that she might, at last, be on the trail of Marcus's family.

"The chile—I think it be a boy—was never seen again," Malinda said evasively.

Sarah waited for her to go on. When she didn't, she asked, "What about the woman? Was she ever seen again?

Oh, Malinda, if only I could find her for Marcus! He would be so . . ."

"Leave it be, chile!" Malinda ordered, heading for the door.

"But she's his wife, Malinda! And Marcus is my friend. He received free papers from his owners, but Dulcie belonged to a different master and was sold with their little boy. Marcus has prayed and searched for them ever since. Even the Governor of Virginia has tried to find them! Oh, wouldn't it be grand if we found them, right here in Kentucky?"

"From what I hear," Malinda said firmly, with her hand on the door latch and her back to Sarah, "it be best if you pray this woman not be the one."

Sarah felt her stubborn streak spreading out. "Where is she, Malinda?" she demanded. "If you know, tell me!"

Malinda turned to face her. "Leave it be, missy," she repeated, and in spite of her bulk, was out the door and gone before Sarah could ask any more questions.

"I believe I could sit on that bench by the fireplace a little while," Ma said a few days later. "I'm that much stronger! I don't know what on earth Malinda has been poking down me, but it surely is working! And just listen to that baby cry! Isn't that a welcome sound? The little thing is hungry and wants the world to know it."

Sarah smiled at Ma as she reached for the little "bottle" Malinda had made from the stretchy membrane of a deer's stomach and filled it with the milk mixture Malinda had shown her how to fix. Then Sarah went over to the baby, picked her up, and stuck the soft end of the homemade bottle into the baby's eager mouth.

Little Elizabeth did seem to be filling out. Her cheeks had rounded some and bore a tinge of color. And she could make her dinner disappear in no time!

Ma sat watching the baby eat. "Malinda has been God's blessing to us, Sarah," she said. "I do believe both Elizabeth and I would be dead by now if it hadn't been for her expert care. She's better than any doctor!" Ma sighed. "I just wish there were some way we could repay what she has done."

"I've been thinking, Ma," Sarah said, propping the baby up in a nest of pillows and covers, "Mrs. Reynolds has been so good to let Malinda come and do for us, and has even furnished the food she has fed you and the baby, often as not. And they really don't need anything we've got. They have everything we do and more, except . . ." She hesitated, not sure that her idea was worth expressing, not wanting Ma to laugh at her.

"Except what, dear?" Ma asked, reaching her finger out to Elizabeth, who grasped it tightly in her tiny hand.

"Well, I learned a lot of things from our tutor back in Williamsburg, things like history and geography and Latin. And Mrs. Reynolds wants her daughters to have a good education, but, of course, girls don't go to school. And, anyway, only the ABCs and simple arithmetic are taught here. Mrs. Reynolds knows how to read and write, but she doesn't seem to be learned in the things Gabrielle taught my cousins and me. I thought maybe I could teach them what I know."

"Why, Sarah, that's a lovely idea!" Ma exclaimed. "I'm strong enough to stay alone now. Jamie's with Betsy most of the time, and the baby . . ."

"Oh, I could take her with me, Ma," Sarah assured her. "She's no trouble at all, and Malinda and the Reynolds girls would help me with her, I'm sure. At least until you're more able, Ma."

"Well, then, all that remains to be done is to make your offer to Mrs. Reynolds," Ma agreed. "I'd be glad to know we could repay a little of our debt to them."

★ Chapter Six ★

And so Sarah became a teacher much before she had expected, spending two hours each afternoon instructing the three older Reynolds children in the rudiments of history, geography, and Latin, as well as in the social graces and household skills she had learned from Gabrielle Gordon and her Aunt Charity.

The girls—ten, nine, and six—reminded her of herself and her two older cousins. The oldest, Felicity, was quick to pick up the household skills, as her cousin Tabitha had been, and Lucy, the youngest, was proving to be adept at the social graces like her cousin Abigail. But it was the middle child, Caroline, who was the better student in the world of books and language. And, as Gabrielle had done with her, Sarah found herself wanting to spend more time with Caroline. She wanted to teach Caroline all the exciting things Gabrielle had taught her about the places and customs of the world beyond the narrow confines of the fort where they now lived.

"Williamsburg must be an exciting place, Sarah," Caroline remarked one day, when Sarah finished telling them about the taverns where her uncle had sometimes taken them to eat; about Bruton Parish Church, where they had worshiped on Sundays; about the palace and its gardens, where Sarah had spent so much time watching the swans and geese on the canal, and enjoying the beautiful flowers her friend Marcus tended so carefully.

"Williamsburg is just a small town compared to some of the places my tutor had been—Paris, France, and London, England, and . . ." Oh, she wished she could remember all the marvelous places and things Gabrielle had described! She wished she had more books, more pictures to show them.

She said as much to Ma the next afternoon as they sat at the table a few minutes after their noon meal, before time for Sarah to go to the Reynolds' cabin. "I need books, Ma, something besides *The Pilgrim's Progress,* Pa's Bible, and Mrs. Reynolds's storybook," she mourned. "And I need maps and pictures! I could teach them so much more if I just had . . ."

"Mrs. Reynolds seems very pleased with what you're doing, Sarah," Ma broke in. "She says trading Malinda's skills for yours a couple of hours a day is well worth it."

She sighed. "I know Malinda has been a pure blessing to us. Your pa won't know what to think when he gets back, the difference in Elizabeth and me is so great. He didn't want to leave, but I insisted. He was so sure this raid would end our major troubles with the Indians, and he wanted so badly to take part in it. I just pretended to be better than I was. And the Larkins promised to look after us."

Sarah gave Ma a quick hug. "Are you sure you can manage the baby by yourself until I get back from the Reynolds' place, Ma?" she asked anxiously.

"Of course, I can!" Ma laughed. "You and Malinda make sure I don't have much else to do. And I enjoy holding her so much!" Tears welled in her eyes. "I was so sure she was going to die, Sarah." She wiped her eyes with one hand and smiled. "And just look at her now!"

Sarah smiled and bent to drop a kiss on the sleeping baby's forehead. "Jamie's with Betsy again, and I'll be back before suppertime. And it's in the kettle, so don't you do a thing but take care of Elizabeth till I get back from the Reynolds' place," she cautioned.

"Oh, go on with you!" Ma scolded. "You and Malinda will have me so spoiled I'll never be good for anything!"

Sarah started out the door, then turned to shake her finger at Ma. "Promise me!" she demanded.

"Oh, I promise," Ma agreed, laughing again.

Sarah stepped onto the path, thinking how good it sounded to hear Ma laugh again. Now if only Pa and Luke would get back safe from the Indian wars, and they would hear word that Nate was safe, life would be back to where it ought to be. Or as close as it could be under the living conditions endured here at Harrodstown.

Harrodstown! she thought scornfully, looking around at the packed-dirt compound behind its log wall, filled with poor, ugly little cabins that did little more than keep them dry. Some town it was! How long before they could go back to Stoney Creek? She didn't even dare dream of Williamsburg!

The gates of the fort were open, and Sarah could see

across the meadow all the way to the edge of the forest where wildflowers beckoned. Suddenly, even the threat of Indians seemed unimportant compared to her need for space, for air that was free of the stench of fowls and horses and too many human beings closed up in too small a space for too long a time.

Apparently the men of the fort felt safe enough to leave the gates open today, and they had turned the horses out into the corral behind the fort. Maybe it would be safe to take a walk, just as far as the edge of the woods.

Should she get Betsy and Jamie and take them with her? She knew Jamie would love a romp in the meadow, but Betsy was different from that first year she and her family had come to settle on Stoney Creek. She seemed so serious and grown up now. She helped out with Jamie a lot, and she was almost as bad as Tabitha had been about her quilting and sewing, about preparing for the home she would have someday.

Well, at least Luke will have a good wife, Sarah thought, *even if I have lost a companion.* Actually, though, there had been no time to share, even if she had wanted to. Taking care of Ma and little Elizabeth and keeping the cabin clean took almost all of her time. And as soon as she had finished cleaning up after one meal, it was time to begin preparing for the next one.

Sarah supposed Ma had worked that way all along. She had helped Ma much of the time, but having to do it all, plus take care of two sick ones, was hard. She was glad Ma and the baby were better now. Just having Ma able to hold and feed Elizabeth, and keep her while Sarah performed her tutoring duties for the Reynolds children helped tremendously.

★ Chapter Six ★

Soon now, she promised herself, *I will be able to get on with my search for Dulcie and Sam.* She had been there two weeks already, and except for quizzing Malinda, she had done nothing to find them. There had been no sign of Indians lately. Surely when Pa or Uncle Ethan came back, they would take her to Boonesborough so she could question the people there about the black woman who had escaped from the Indians.

From the height of the sun in the sky, Sarah judged that it was nearly time for her afternoon lessons with the Reynolds girls. She sighed. There wasn't time for her to take that longed-for walk in the meadow . . . unless she could persuade Mrs. Reynolds to let her take the girls on a trip across the clearing. She could teach them about trees and wildflowers. She could show them how to make patterns for their embroidery from leaves and blossoms, and they might even find some insects to study, some bees and bugs and butterflies, as she and her cousins had studied with Gabrielle.

"Well, it is a beautiful day," Mrs. Reynolds said hesitantly when Sarah proposed her plan. She threw a questioning glance at Malinda, but the silent woman kept her eyes on the baby in her lap. "I understand that some of the men took their wives out to milk the cows at the edge of the forest this morning. I don't suppose they've seen any Indian sign lately." A frown creased her pretty forehead and troubled her cornflower blue eyes. "Still, there was no sign the day my husband was killed, either, no warning at all. What if? . . ."

"We'd be very careful," Sarah promised. "We wouldn't go into the woods, just to the edge to pick flowers, and we'd keep a sharp lookout for trouble."

"Please, Ma!" the three girls begged in unison. "Please let us go with Sarah!"

"I believe I'll go crazy if I don't get out of this fort for a few minutes!" Felicity added fervently.

Sarah smiled. She knew just how the eleven year old felt.

Mrs. Reynolds looked from one of her daughters to the other. "Oh, all right," she agreed. "Just for a little while."

The girls squealed with delight and danced around Sarah, then danced out the door.

They were on their way. Sarah took a deep breath as they walked through the open gates into the clearing. How good it felt to be where there were no walls to shut her in, unless she counted the thick wall of trees across 300 yards of open space.

The way the meadow ran right up to the dark fringe of trees reminded her of their place on Stoney Creek. Would Pa go back there? Would he start all over to build a farm there? Even if he rebuilt everything, after the terrible destruction the Indians had brought upon them, would they ever feel safe there again?

Well, she had never felt safe there anyway! But after being cooped up in the fort for several weeks, she was ready to take her chances on wilderness and Indians. It seemed they had been shut up behind those log walls forever!

"Race you to the trees!" Lucy called.

Sarah joined the three girls as, laughing, they ran wildly across the meadow.

"Oh, Sarah, look!" Caroline exclaimed. "There's a columbine! Look how the little upside-down blooms dangle from the stems, and, oh, what a bright, pretty red and yellow it is!"

"I like vi'lets best," Lucy said firmly. "Little purple vi'lets all hugged up in a nest of green leaves."

"I'd like to find some greens for supper," Felicity said. "Some mustard, and maybe some wild pokeweed. Ma loves wild pokeweed. But I guess it's too late for it now. The stems would be bitter."

"It gets poison when it gets old, Felicity," Caroline reminded her. "You have to get it when it first comes through the ground."

"Here are some ripe blackberries," Sarah called, and the girls eagerly joined her to pick and eat the welcome sweets.

Then, lips stained purple from blackberry juice, they hunted acorns, and Sarah showed them how to make doll dishes out of them for a playhouse.

They were having such a good time, Sarah forgot to notice the time until a rain crow sent its plaintive "ooo-ahh-ooo" straight down her spine. She looked around, surprised to see that the sun had already traveled behind the fort. The sky was still light, but fireflies were beginning to flicker over the meadow.

"Ooo-ahh-ooo!" The cry reminded Sarah of a night in the forest when she and Luke and Pa had gone to take honey from a bee tree, and suddenly the cries of whip-poorwills and rain crows had surrounded them. Pa had said later that he knew it was time to head for home because the bird cries kept getting closer, and there were too many of them.

Was this one lonely call truly the cry of a rusty-colored rain crow warning of rain? Or was it a skilled imitation done by a clever Indian calling to his friends? Sarah searched the nearby tree limbs, but saw no bird. It should be easy to see, for the rain crow was bigger than a robin, bigger than a mockingbird even, and not much smaller than a regular old black crow.

"Come on, bird!" Sarah begged. "Show yourself!"

"Ooo-ahh-ooo!" Again, the cry shivered through the forest and down Sarah's spine. Was it closer this time? Still, there was only one.

"What's wrong, Sarah?" Caroline asked. Felicity straightened up from her search for greens, her wide gray eyes going from Sarah to Caroline and back again.

"I'm not sure," Sarah answered quietly.

"Ooo-ahh-ooo, coo-coo-coo!" The cry was closer this time. She was sure of it. Sarah reached down and took Lucy's hand.

★ Chapter Seven ★

"Is it the bird calls?" Caroline whispered.

Sarah nodded. "Let's get back to the fort," she said. "Pretend to pick flowers into the meadow until we get closer to the stockade. Then, when I yell, 'Run!' race like the wind for the gates."

Lucy gave a low whimper, and Sarah squeezed her hand reassuringly. "Don't act scared," she warned, trying to remember Pa's way of dealing with danger. "Anyway, it's probably just a little old rain crow calling," she added. "I just don't want to take any chances."

She plucked a daisy from its stem, then another and another, quickly working her way into the wide expanse of unprotected meadow, still holding tightly to little Lucy's trembling hand. Out of the corner of her eye, she could see Felicity and Caroline snatching daisies from their stems, edging closer and closer to the fort.

"Ooo-ahh-ooo, coo-coo-coo!" The sound seemed to come from the very edge of the forest, but Sarah didn't dare look back. "Run!" she hissed, jerking Lucy along beside her as she ran for the gates just behind the other girls, the sound of their running feet pounding against the hot, heavy silence.

Suddenly, there was a cry from the fort and the report of a gun rang out, followed by a whole volley of shots. Sarah heard a grunt behind her, and the soft padding sound she had thought was their own feet stopped. She threw a glance behind her, and felt her heart lurch with terror. Three war-painted Indians had turned at the shots and were running back toward the forest, one of them limping as he ran. She glimpsed two more dark shapes back among the trees.

"Oh, run, Lucy!" she urged, tugging at the little girl's hand, trying to shield her with her own body, expecting any moment to feel an arrow between her shoulder blades.

The gates were swinging shut as she flung Lucy through the opening behind her sisters and dived around the gate herself.

One of the men secured the gates with the heavy bar that lay across them. "Are ye all right, little gals?" he asked. "One of them savages was ready to grab you two when Zeke shot him in the leg!" he said to Sarah and Lucy. "It's a good thing that woman of Mrs. Reynolds gave the warning. You'd a been a goner for sure! Are ye all right?" he repeated.

Sarah nodded, gasping for breath. "I . . . I think so," she finally managed to gasp.

Mrs. Reynolds ran to draw her hysterical children into her arms. "Thank God you're safe! When I heard the guns . . . Oh, thank God!" she babbled.

"The cattle!" a man shouted from the walkway built up on the wall. "The ornery rascals have got two cows and a calf!"

Again, gunfire rang out above Sarah's head. Across the meadow, a cow bawled loudly.

A woman flew past Sarah and threw herself at the gate, clawing at the bar. "That's Flossie!" she cried. "They can't have Flossie!"

A man grabbed her by the arms and dragged her away from the gates. "Ma'am, you can't go out there!" he said. "It'd be certain death! No cow's worth what you would face out there!"

The woman struggled briefly, then sank down, hid her face in her apron, and began to sob, rocking back and forth on the ground. Outside the stockade, a cow bawled and was answered by a calf.

The man laid his hand on her shoulder. "I'm sorry,

ma'am," he said. "I reckon we shouldn't have let the cattle roam the woods," he explained to no one in particular. "But they need pasture, and there ain't been any Indian sign to speak of for weeks now."

"I think they're leaving," one of the men on the wall called down to them. "They've melted into the trees, cows and all."

"Just a small party, I think," another man added. "They likely won't be back, leastways not till after dark."

"We'll have to get the horses and the rest of the cattle inside before then," the first man said. "If the horses hadn't been so close to the fort, I reckon the savages would have gotten them, too."

"None of us can afford to lose any livestock!" another man said.

"None of us can afford to lose anything," said a woman, coming to comfort the first woman on the ground who began to sob again.

Sarah saw Mrs. Reynolds leading her daughters toward their cabin and ran after them. "I'm so sorry!" she panted. "Oh, Mrs. Reynolds, if anything had happened to one of them . . ."

Mrs. Reynolds stopped and turned to face Sarah, her arms still tightly holding her children. She nodded. "I know how you feel, Sarah," she said. "I shouldn't have let them go. It was just such a pretty day, and danger seemed so far away, like nothing bad could happen on such a day." She patted Sarah's hand. "I just thank God you're all back safe. But don't ever ask me to let them go outside the fort again, because I never, never will!" She turned and headed across the compound.

Sarah stood watching them go. She knew Mrs. Reynolds

had lost her husband in an Indian raid. What if, because of her, the little girls had been killed or captured? She shivered and turned to make her way to their own cabin.

Then Sarah gasped as Malinda appeared beside her. "Malinda, you walk just like a cat!" she said, laughing shakily. "Or an Indian! I never know you're around until there you are!"

"That be a close call you and the little misses had," Malinda said seriously.

Sarah nodded. "Thank you for sounding the alarm. How did you know the Indians were there? Were you watching from one of those little square holes the men shoot out of in the blockhouses?" There were no other windows that faced outside the compound where attacking Indians could slip inside.

"Oh, I be watching," Malinda answered evasively. "How did you know the Indians were there? What told you to head the girls back to the fort all of a sudden?"

"I heard the rain crows," Sarah answered, shuddering at the thought of how close they had come to a violent death or to capture, which might have been worse. "When I heard two of them, and they were moving closer, I decided it was time to get back inside the fort!"

Malinda nodded approvingly. "It's a good thing you did!" she said. "That Indian was ready to grab you and Lucy. If he hadn't been hit in the leg with that bullet, you'd likely be his squaw."

"Malinda!" she gasped. "I never would be!"

Malinda's dark eyes grew sober. "You would have no choice, little miss. That's likely what happened to your Dulcie," she added.

Sarah couldn't believe the woman had brought up the

subject of Dulcie herself. She always seemed so reluctant to talk about her.

"So that was Dulcie! Tell me about her, Malinda, please!" Sarah begged. "Tell me all you know."

Malinda studied her seriously. "They say she be as slender and graceful as one of those white and purple flags blooming in Mrs. Butler's chimney corner over there," she said dreamily. "They say she had hair and eyes as black as a crow's wing."

She paused, and Sarah struggled to control her impatience, fearing Malinda would stop talking if she broke the mood.

"They say her hair turned white, missy," Malinda went on, her voice lower now. "It turned solid white between the time she be captured and the time, just a few months later, when she came limping into Boonesborough."

Malinda turned and began to walk toward the cabins, and Sarah skipped a step or two to catch up with her. "Where is she now, Malinda?" she asked.

"They say she eat a little, sleep a little. But she never say a word. And when she look you straight in the eyes, it be like looking in the windows of an empty house," Malinda continued, her gaze fixed somewhere over the roof of the closest cabin.

"Do you know where she is, Malinda?" Sarah repeated.

"I just be glad you and the little misses weren't captured," Malinda said, her voice normal now and her manner brisk. She would not meet Sarah's eyes.

"Malinda . . ." Sarah began impatiently.

"Good night, Miss Sarah," Malinda said firmly, turning down toward the Reynolds' cabin.

Sarah sighed. Obviously, she wasn't going to get any

more information out of the stubborn woman this evening.

"Good night, Malinda," she said resignedly.

Sarah supposed she'd just have to get to Boonesborough before she could find out anything more. But with the Indians around again, how could she get there? It wouldn't do Marcus—or Dulcie and Sam—any good for her to lie dead out there in the forest or to spend the rest of her days as an Indian squaw!

When Pa and Uncle Ethan came back, maybe she could persuade them to help her find Dulcie. Uncle Ethan was very fond of Marcus. If neither of them would help, she vowed as she stepped up into the cabin doorway, she would find a way.

"Sarah!" Ma exclaimed. "Where have you been?" She was sitting on the edge of the bed, holding the baby. "I've been so worried! I heard gunfire," she said.

Sarah swallowed hard, trying to collect her scattered thoughts, knowing she had to explain to Ma about her foolish escapade outside the stockade and why gunfire had shattered the peace of the once beautiful afternoon.

The next morning, it was as though there had never been Indians anywhere around the fort. After sending scouts into the forest and finding no Indian sign, the men turned the horses back into the corral and the cattle back out to forage for food.

Sarah fixed Ma's breakfast and fed Elizabeth, then decided to visit Jamie. She couldn't just let him become a member of the Larkin family. He was her little brother!

"I've got to find a way to win back Jamie's affections!" she told Ma as she put the clean dishes back on the shelf. "He acts like I'm a complete stranger!"

"Give him time, Sarah," Ma advised. "He was heartbroken when you left. Then he learned to live without you. It's a way little children have of dealing with grief. They just close their lives over a loss like water fills a hole. You're a stranger to him now, but if you will be patient, I am sure you can win him back to you."

★ Reunion in Kentucky ★

Suddenly Sarah had an inspiration. She had forgotten the little nonpareils she had brought from Williamsburg for Jamie and Luke! In fact, with Ma and the baby so ill, she had forgotten all of her gifts for the family. Rummaging in the deerskin bag, she pulled out the cinnamon sticks and the horn comb and handed them to Ma.

"Why, thank you, Sarah!" Ma exclaimed. "The teeth in my old comb are almost as scarce as hens' teeth!" She laughed. "And the carving of the horn they used to make this one is so pretty!" Then she sniffed at the cinnamon. "My, I don't know when I've had cinnamon to flavor anything!" she added.

"I brought some things for Pa and Luke, too," Sarah said, taking the parcel of nonpareils out of the bag and untying the twine that held it. She handed Ma one of the little chocolate candies, then slipped a handful of them into her apron pocket. "I'm going to see Jamie," she explained.

Jamie and Ruthie were busy building a farm out of corncobs, the way Luke used to do. Sarah supposed Luke had taught the little fellow that game. She watched as Jamie played with the little donkey Luke had carved as part of the nativity scene he had made for their first Christmas on Stoney Creek.

She stood there remembering how Jamie had immediately claimed the little donkey as his own and had run all over the cabin with it in his hand, yelling, "Hossie! Hossie!" Those had been happy days, even if she had spent most of them longing to be back in Virginia. At least the family had been together, all except Nate off fighting in the Revolution, and everybody had been well.

Betsy looked up and smiled at her. "Come on in, Sarah," she invited. "Jamie, it's Sarah," she said.

Jamie looked up at her solemnly, then went on playing with Ruthie.

Sarah went over and knelt down in front of him. "I brought you something from Williamsburg, Jamie," she tempted, holding out one of the nonpareils. "It's candy," she explained, putting one into her mouth and eating it to show him what it was. "They're called nonpareils," she explained to Betsy, handing her one. "Our tutor in Williamsburg said the name is French and means 'unequaled,' and they surely are! Nonpareils are the best!"

Jamie stared at her warily, then got up and ran over to where Betsy sat mending a sock.

"Sarah's brought you something good to eat, Jamie," Betsy encouraged. "Go see what it is!" But the little boy edged over against her, clutching her skirt with one hand, as he had done that first night.

★ Reunion in Kentucky ★

Ruthie came over, and Sarah put one of the little chocolates into her hand. Ruthie bit into it, and a big grin spread over her face. She popped the rest of her piece into her mouth, chewed, and swallowed. Then she stood looking at Sarah, begging with her big blue eyes for more.

"Here you go, Ruthie," Sarah said, handing her one for each hand. "I reckon Jamie doesn't want any."

Jamie cast a longing look at the candy in Sarah's hand, then looked up at Betsy pleadingly. Betsy handed him her piece of candy. Jamie stuck it in his mouth whole and began to chew. Then he closed his eyes, his little face registering the pleasure he found in the unaccustomed treat.

Sarah handed Betsy a handful of the candies. "Some for him and some for you and Ruthie," she said, turning to go before Betsy could see the tears her little brother's continued rejection brought to her eyes.

"I'll bring him home after supper," Betsy promised, her face flushed with the awkwardness of the situation. "He'll get used to you again."

"Give him time, Sarah. He'll come around," Mrs. Larkin said encouragingly from over by the fireplace, echoing Ma's words of earlier that morning. "How's your ma today, and the baby?" she changed the subject.

"Better, thank you, Mrs. Larkin," Sarah answered, trying not to think about Jamie and his reaction to her. "That Malinda has just worked wonders with both of them! I thank God we found her!"

Mrs. Larkin nodded. "The Lord works in mysterious ways sometimes. I'm thinking on asking her to take a look at Mark's leg. He's up hobbling around on it, but it just won't heal right. You know, I think those Indian arrows have some kind of poison on them. Do you think she would be willing to see what she could do for him?"

"Why don't you just ask her?" Sarah suggested. "I'm sure she'll help. I'll see you tonight, Betsy," she added as she left the cabin. Then she called back, "You, too, Jamie!"

Later that day, Sarah saw Mrs. Larkin go down to the blockhouse and head inside. When she came out, Malinda was with her. Malinda didn't come to their cabin that evening, but they really didn't need her any longer. Ma was so much better, and the baby was thriving. Now, if she could just get Jamie back!

Betsy brought him home just before dark, and, at her urging, he went dutifully over to the bed to give Ma a hug. Sarah supposed he felt strange with Ma, too, since she had been sick for so long and unable to care for him. And when Betsy tried to leave, he cried so hard Betsy had to lie down on the trundle bed with him until he went to sleep. When he finally dozed off, Sarah eased into Betsy's place, holding her breath for fear he would awaken and begin to scream again.

The next morning, Jamie watched Sarah with solemn eyes as she fixed breakfast. Then he let her help him dress. He didn't ask for Betsy, but he kept looking around the room as though he missed something. Sarah could see the tears threatening.

"Eat your breakfast, sweets, and I'll take you over to play with Ruthie in a little while," she promised.

When they left the cabin, Jamie turned to give Ma a wave and a sad little smile that broke Sarah's heart. But when she left him at the Larkins, he was laughing aloud as he and Ruthie added a barn to their miniature corncob farm.

★ Reunion in Kentucky ★

Even as the hurt twisted painfully inside her, Sarah knew she couldn't blame the little fellow for feeling the way he did. He had practically been her baby for three years. Then she had left him, and in his loneliness, he had become attached to the Larkins. She sighed. Somehow, she had to find a way back into his heart.

All afternoon, as she listened to the Reynolds girls practice their reading from the Book of Proverbs, she tried to think of a way to win back Jamie's affections, but no solution came to her. These readings proclaimed patience as a virtue, and, as Ma and Mrs. Larkin had advised, she supposed she would just have to be patient.

As she left the Reynolds cabin, Sarah noticed that the stockade gates were open. Could she risk taking a walk, just outside the walls this time so she could get back inside quickly if danger appeared? She wouldn't cross the meadow. She would just go around the gates into the cemetery.

There are so many graves here! she thought, moving slowly among the rough stones that marked the grave spaces without recalling the names of those buried there. It seemed a lot of deaths for the short time Harrodstown had been here. The beautiful land required a heavy sacrifice of those who would settle it. Many of the headstones and footstones were close together, indicating that a child lay between them. Had it not been for Malinda, Sarah acknowledged gratefully, little Elizabeth might also lie in this sad place.

Sarah shivered in the hot sunshine and forced her thoughts to happier things—the graceful way the tall meadow grasses danced in the soft breeze, the sound of water laughing its way down a rocky creek bed, the trills of a wild canary singing in the woods. She sat down, leaned her back against an ancient oak, and closed her eyes, absorbing the drowsy peace of a summer afternoon without threat of illness or death.

It was hard to believe that on such a beautiful afternoon she couldn't just ride Gracie across the meadow and through the forest straight to Boonesborough. Sarah was convinced that the clues to Dulcie's whereabouts were at Boonesborough, but she didn't even know how to get there. And there was nobody at Harrodstown whom she could ask to take her. Even if Pa or Uncle Ethan were there, they might not think the trip was worth the dangers involved.

Marcus had been the only one willing to ride the dark road to Norfolk with her in search of Gabrielle. Marcus. Her special friend. How many times had he comforted her? How many times had he dried her tears? She reached into her pocket and touched the blue handkerchief. She could almost see his sad, dark eyes and hear his deep, musical voice as he told her some story that would shed light on a problem.

If she had a purpose on this earth, it surely was to find Dulcie and Sam and reunite them with this kind, gentle man who loved them so.

"If God knows and cares when a tiny sparrow falls to the ground, you know he's watching out for folks," Marcus had said that day in the gardens when she had been so worried about Ma. Surely God was looking out for Marcus's wife and son!

Was He though? Did God really care about individual people down here on earth? Or was that just something Marcus wanted to believe? Did God care what happened to Dulcie and Sam? Did Marcus's heartbreak concern Him? Could she really trust Him to watch over Pa and Luke at the Indian villages, over Nate out there fighting the British?

Just before she left Williamsburg, Marcus had told her to trust in the Lord with all her heart. "But how, Marcus?" she whispered. "How can I trust someone I don't even know? I believe in Him, but I just don't know God like you and Pa do! I don't even know how to get to know Him!"

Then a new thought came to Sarah. She might not know God, but God knew everything. He knew where Dulcie was this very moment!

"Dear God," she whispered fervently, "I don't know You very well, but Marcus does, and he's trusting You to find Dulcie. Please show me where she is. And Sam, too. Please help me get them back for Marcus! And, like it says in the Book of Proverbs, I'll try to be patient until You do." Then she added, "Only please don't take too long!"

When Sarah finally got up and went back inside the fort, the sun was ending its journey down the western sky, and Betsy was just leaving the Larkin cabin to bring Jamie home.

Betsy stayed while he ate his supper. He let Sarah undress him and get him ready for bed, keeping his eyes fixed on Betsy all the while. His lip trembled when Betsy said good night and left, but Sarah quickly handed him one of her dwindling store of nonpareils, and he didn't cry.

When he had finished eating and she had wiped the chocolate from his lips, she helped him onto the trundle bed and lay down beside him. She took his hand. "The little baby birds are asleep in their nests, with their mother's wings spread over them," she said softly, beginning the story she had told him countless times when he was younger and she was trying to get him to sleep. "And the little squirrels are asleep in their holes in the hollow trees with their fluffy tails wrapped around them."

She heard Jamie sniff, as though he might be crying silently.

"The little rabbits are asleep in their cozy burrows beneath the roots of the big trees," she went on, "and the little mice are asleep all piled on top of each other in their holes in the meadow grass," she whispered in his ear, feeling his little body beginning to relax against her. "The little deer is asleep in the cedar thicket with his mother. And the little boys are asleep in their beds with their families sleeping all around them," she said, resisting the urge to hug him in her gladness to have him home. "The little . . ." Then she heard him breathing deeply and knew that he had fallen asleep.

Had he recognized the little story they had shared so often? Sarah hoped so. Tomorrow she would try to find time to do something special with him, as they used to do back on Stoney Creek when he had toddled after her almost everywhere.

Sarah lay awake in the hot August evening, grateful for her little brother's return, for Ma's and the baby's improvement, for the hint of a cooling breeze that blew from the door across the cabin to the window.

Outside, a screech owl called, and a fox screamed, sounding just like a woman. Deep in the forest, a whip-poorwill cried.

"Ten o'clock, and all is well!" the sentry called.

It was good to know he was on duty, Sarah thought, drifting into sleep. She didn't awaken until she heard guns exploding all around her.

9

"Lord, have mercy upon us!" Ma breathed.

"What is it, Ma? Indians?" Sarah asked.

Elizabeth awoke and began to cry. Jamie sat up, rubbing his eyes sleepily. "Don't cwy, baby!" he ordered sternly.

Sarah got up and dressed quickly. She picked up Elizabeth and laid her beside Jamie. "Talk to her, Jamie," she said. "I'm going to see what's going on."

"Sarah, be careful!" Ma called, getting up slowly and reaching for her dress.

Sarah stood in the doorway a moment. She could see the men on the stockade firing and reloading their guns. But what were they trying to shoot? They were aiming straight up in the sky!

She slipped outside and edged along the path toward the front of the compound. Then she saw the gates swing open, and a large band of men on horseback rode inside.

"They're back!" one man called, scrambling down from

the wall. "Hey, everybody! The men are back from the Indian wars!" Another volley of shots went off.

"You'd better save that powder and lead for the Indians!" someone yelled.

The newcomers were dismounting and being greeted by the men of the fort with slaps on the back and even a few quick bear hugs. Sarah tried to see through the milling crowd. Then she gasped. She began to run, then turned back toward the cabin.

"Ma! Ma! It's Pa and Luke!" she called, running inside. "They're home!" She grabbed Jamie up in her arms and ran out again.

"Pa!" she cried. "Oh, Pa, it's so good to see you!"

"Sary?" he questioned, dismounting. Then he caught her to him in a hug. "Where did you? . . . How on earth did you get here?"

"Uncle Ethan brought me," she explained.

"Ethan's here?" he asked, looking at the faces clustered around them.

"No, he's gone on now to complete some task for the Patriots," she explained. "I haven't seen him since he dropped me off here."

"How's Della?" Pa asked anxiously.

"Ma's much better, Pa," Sarah assured him, "and little Elizabeth is beginning to grow."

"Praise God!" he breathed. "I was so afraid of what I would hear when I got back, but I felt I had to go on this expedition to make our home safe for all of us."

"I reckon you got my letter," a familiar voice said, coming up beside them. "How's Ma and the baby?"

"Luke!" Sarah cried, grabbing her brother's hand then throwing her arms around him. "I hardly knew you! You've grown so . . . big!" she finished, gasping for breath as he returned her hug.

"I can see you're all right, fellow," Luke said to Jamie, giving him a playful little punch on the shoulder. Jamie grinned and ducked his head shyly.

"You're getting to be a big boy, too, aren't you?" Pa said, lifting Jamie up over his head, making the little boy laugh aloud.

"We captured two Indian villages without even firing a shot!" Luke bragged as he removed a bedroll from behind his saddle.

"Oh, Luke, stop your teasing . . . " Sarah began.

"No, I'm serious," Luke insisted. "We did, didn't we, Pa? Colonel Clark has taken 'em all as prisoners to Fort Pitt!"

Pa nodded. "We completely surprised them. The rascals surrendered without a fight," he called back on his way to the cabin where Ma and Elizabeth waited in the doorway.

That was only the first two times Sarah heard the story of the surrender of the Indian villages "without a shot." As the day wore on, it was told over and over with various embellishments, by first one returning hero, then another. But she didn't mind. It was so good to have them home! And the fact that a major source of their troubles here on the frontier had been reduced by the capture of so many Indians, more than justified the celebration the people of Harrodstown were preparing.

The fort was a bustling place that morning under the burning August sun. Sarah could almost imagine that she was walking down busy Duke of Gloucester Street amid a throng of holiday shoppers! She could smell the roasting deer and wild turkey, and her mouth watered as she picked and strung green beans and peeled new potatoes to boil with them in the iron kettle over the fire.

Mrs. Larkin and Betsy were baking sweet potato pies. The Carsons were shucking and silking ears of corn for roasting. The Reynolds ladies, under the watchful eye of Malinda, were stirring up batch after batch of biscuits. And almost every household had a pot of beans and potatoes cooking, for it would take a lot of food to feed their conquering army. Thank goodness some of Colonel Clark's men had gone on to Fort Pitt with their captives!

Sarah stood back to admire the tables they had set outside. With every family sharing what dishes and utensils they had, the tables looked fit for a banquet, and the heaping bowls and platters of food looked like they were about to have one.

"Are those men going to sit around the tables all night?" Betsy whispered as they washed and dried yet another pile of dirty dishes. "I'm starved!"

Sarah wiped her steaming face on her apron. "I hope they don't eat all the drumsticks!" she said fervently.

When the men finally arose and walked away from the tables, Sarah grabbed five clean plates, handed two of them to Betsy for her and Ruthie, and filled two for Ma and Jamie, giving her little brother the last drumstick.

"Oh, well, I like turkey breast, too," she said to Betsy as they dropped down under the sweet gum tree to eat. "I'm so hungry, as Luke says, I could eat a cow fried in gravy!"

"Where is Luke?" Betsy asked, searching the cluster of men with eager eyes.

★ Chapter Nine ★

"I don't know," Sarah answered indifferently around her last mouthful of biscuit. "I noticed he put away his share of Malinda's biscuits and Mrs. Larkin's pie! Let's go see if he left any pie for us," she suggested. "Betsy?" She turned to see why Betsy hadn't answered her, and discovered that she had disappeared. Then Sarah located her, sitting with Luke on the front stoop of a nearby cabin.

Sarah rolled her eyes in disgust and went off seeking pie on her own. One piece of sweet potato pie later, she sighed contentedly, then pushed herself up from the ground and began to collect Ma's dishes.

The men were singing now, some rousing marching song, and mothers were calling their smaller children in to bed. Quickly, Sarah washed and dried Ma's dishes and carried them into the cabin, past Jamie who was sitting on the stoop, trying to prop his drooping eyelids open with his fingers.

Sarah saw that Ma had fed Elizabeth and, exhausted from the unaccustomed activities of the day, had gone to bed with her. Sarah dressed Jamie for bed, knowing there would be no need for bedtime stories tonight. The little fellow was asleep almost before his head touched the pillow.

She stood in the cabin doorway, watching the Reynolds girls and other children chasing fireflies across the compound, but she didn't have the energy to join them.

She saw Betsy and Luke, having given up all pretense of interest in other people, strolling hand in hand around the stockade.

Sarah sank down on the stoop where Jamie had been, and listened to the men recounting their days of marching through the mud and the wilderness to Kaskaskia and then

89

to Cahokia. They marveled at the brilliance of George Rogers Clark's military strategies and the success of their campaign. And underneath it all, Sarah could detect a sense of relief that they had all returned home without loss.

"There's plenty more of the red devils out there," she heard one man say, "but we sure got rid of a bunch of 'em!"

"Wonder how that Indian scout felt about helping us locate those villages and capture his friends," another commented.

"They may have been his enemies," someone else answered. "Leastways, I don't think they were from his tribe."

"The Little Captain is very proud that he works for 'General S'washington,' as he calls him," Pa put in, chuckling. "He's quick to point out that he wears a blue coat, not a red one."

Sarah remembered the Little Captain. He was the Indian Ma had fed the first night they camped on their new land on Stoney Creek. To thank her, he had given Ma his silver necklace. Sarah was convinced that wearing that necklace had saved Ma's life the day other Indians attacked their cabin. Since then, Ma had always worn it.

"Yes sir, the Little Captain is one Indian who has no love for the British!" Pa was saying.

"I didn't get the impression he was all that fond of us, neither!" someone said, causing a round of laughter.

"He's a friend of Daniel Boone," Pa pointed out.

"Boone's got too many Indian friends, to my way of thinking," another man spat out angrily.

"I reckon you fellers had already left to go meet Colonel Clark, so you may not know that Boone escaped from those Indians who captured him and his men back in February," one of the men who had stayed at the fort remarked.

The angry man snorted. "Boone talked 'em into surrendering to his Indian friends, you mean."

"He says it was to save their lives," the first man insisted. "And the Indians kept their word, let all of them go but Boone. Anyway," he went on, "Boone overheard the Indians plotting to attack Boonesborough with over 400 braves, so he escaped—sometime in early June, I think it was—and traveled 160 miles afoot in ten days to sound the alarm."

"That's his story!" the angry man retorted. "I still say ole Dan'l comes and goes a bit too freely amongst those Indians."

"The Indians didn't show up, though," the first speaker went on. "I reckon they knew with Boone gone, the forts would be ready for them."

"Shoot!" somebody else exclaimed. "There ain't more than twenty-five men at Boonesborough! What could they do against so many Indians?"

"Don't count on that threat being over, anyway," a voice Sarah hadn't heard yet cautioned. "They're likely just lying low till the warning wears off. They'll come, mark my words, and when we least expect it!"

"I expect I'd better be heading for bed," another broke in with a yawn. "I don't know about you fellers, but I'm worn down to a frazzle!"

The men laughed, and Sarah saw them getting up and heading for their cabins and the blockhouses where the single men stayed.

"Betsy!" Sarah heard Mrs. Larkin call, and soon after

that Luke came into their cabin. He unrolled his bedroll and lay down on the floor by the unlit fireplace. Soon she heard him snoring.

Pa came in, patting her on the shoulder as he passed. "It's good to have you back, Sary girl," he said.

"I'm glad to be back, Pa," she answered automatically. Then she put her hand to her mouth. Had she just lied to Pa? Or was she really glad to be back in the wilderness, preparing to go to bed on a lumpy straw mattress instead of getting ready to crawl into Meggie's thick, fluffy feather bed? Instead of spending the night in a quiet, cool, tall-ceilinged room shared with one little girl, was she really glad to bed down here with six people in this cramped, stuffy little room?

Well, I am glad to have my family all around me again, even if my father and my brother do snore! she thought, covering her ears with the pillow.

She lay there, her mind whirling with the events of the past few hours. It had been a busy, exciting day, from the moment she was awakened by gun shots until the end of the feasting and festivities tonight. She was exhausted! Her bones felt like they could sink right through that pitiful excuse for a mattress. But she couldn't seem to fall asleep. She reckoned maybe she was just too tired to go to sleep.

Sarah slipped quietly out of bed and went back to sit in the doorway. The night was hot and heavy with silence. Was Dulcie out there somewhere, searching for her lost son as Marcus had searched all these years?

Somewhere out there, Sam wandered with the Indians. The men had said nothing about seeing a black captive among the Indians they had taken prisoner, but there were other villages, other tribes. Somewhere Sam waited for rescue. Did he miss his mother and his father? Did he even remember Marcus? It had been a long time since he had seen his father.

Sarah listened. The silence was deep, complete. No night birds called. No animals cried out back in the forest. There was something threatening, something eerie about this night, she thought, as she crept back into bed. It was as though the silence waited.

Sarah sat up and listened. She slipped out of bed and stood in the open doorway.

There it was again—an eerie drumming sound down in the forest. That was what had awakened her.

"What is it, Sarah?" Ma whispered from the bed. "Are the Indians back? Where's your pa?"

"I don't know, Ma," Sarah said in answer to all three questions. "Did you hear that noise?"

Ma got up and began to dress. Sarah whipped off her own gown and slipped on her dress.

"Should I get Jamie dressed, too?" she whispered.

"Not yet," Ma breathed. "The fort is solid. It's withstood attack several times. Just a handful of men can defend a place as well fortified as Harrodstown."

"I've never known the Indians to warn their victims by playing the tom-toms before they attack," Pa said from outside the door. "But why else would they be out there?"

"Tom-toms?" Sarah repeated.

"They're a kind of drum the Indians make out of wood and animal skins," he explained. "They usually play them in their villages when they are trying to get their braves excited about a coming battle."

Sarah shivered despite the heat.

Pa came inside. "Well, I've heard tom-toms before, and I'm not going to let them ruin my sleep. We have guards posted. If the Indians come, we will be warned. I'm going back to bed. What about the rest of you?"

"I'm with you, Pa," Luke said, stumbling sleepily back to his pallet before the cold fireplace.

"In a minute, Pa," Sarah said. "I've never heard these drums before. Anyway, I don't think I could sleep right now."

"Suit yourself, Sary girl," he said, yawning. "But stay near the cabin."

"You don't need to worry about that!" she agreed.

Suddenly the drums stopped, leaving a hole in the darkness. Sarah's ears throbbed with the remembered rhythm, but not even the cry of a bird or animal broke the heavy silence. The world seemed to hold its breath, waiting for whatever would come next.

Sarah was about to head back to bed, then she froze. Something moved down by the spring. She strained her eyes to see in the darkness. Then she saw it again—a shadow among the shadows, gliding silently along the back stockade wall toward George Rogers Clark's blockhouse where Malinda and the Reynoldses lay sleeping.

I have to warn them! she thought, running out the door, her bare feet padding down the path toward the open door of the corner building.

★ Chapter Ten ★

Suddenly realizing her danger, Sarah threw a terrified glance down toward the spring, then all around the stockade. Nothing moved. Even the leaves of the sweet gum tree over by the animal pen hung motionless in the hot, still air.

Where had the menacing shadow gone? He hadn't entered the blockhouse. He would have had to pass right in front of her to do so. Where was he?

Sarah looked around for something to shelter her from whatever lurked out there in the darkness, but there was nothing, not even a tree trunk. All the trees inside the compound had been cut down so that Indians could not slip inside the fort and hide in them. There was just that one old sweet gum tree that shaded the animals toward the front of the fort and two young saplings this side of the spring. She inched her way back toward her family's cabin.

97

"What are you doing out here, missy?" a voice said in her ear.

Sarah jumped and let out a small scream. "Malinda!" she hissed. "You scared me half to death! How did you get right here beside me without me seeing you?"

Malinda chuckled softly, but she said nothing.

"Did you see someone down by the spring just now?" Sarah asked.

"That be me. I heard the drum," the woman answered.

"Drum? You mean drums," Sarah corrected. "The forest must be full of Indians!"

"May be," Malinda agreed. "There be only one drummer, though," she insisted.

"Who goes there?" a sentry called, and Sarah's spine tingled as she heard the cocking of a gun.

"It's Sarah Moore!" she answered quickly, "And Malinda."

"Sarah, are you all right?" Ma called softly from inside the cabin.

"Yes, Ma," Sarah replied.

"What are you doing prowling around out there?" the sentry asked gruffly. "Get back in your cabins before you get shot. Or scalped," he added. "Didn't you hear the drums out there?"

"Thank you, sir," Malinda said quickly. "We be going back inside now, knowing you be so careful on the watch." Sarah felt Malinda's hand on her arm, heading her back toward the cabin.

"Down in Barbados," Malinda murmured, "sometimes the voodoo drums beat all night long, for nights on end! The darkness fairly trembles with their threat. It's enough to make the blood run cold! This little old tom-tom is nothing compared to the witch doctors' drums!"

"This one's enough to make my blood run cold!" Sarah said, shivering.

"That drum out there tonight be nothing to fear, missy," Malinda said. "Just somebody sending a message. There be no threat, not from that drummer."

"How do you know, Malinda?" she asked as they stopped in front of the cabin doorway. "How on earth could you possibly know what those Indians are saying by the beat of their tom-toms?"

"Oh, the words be there, missy," Malinda assured her, "if you be knowing the language. Every beat of the drum be a word or words."

"You mean you know what that drum is saying?" Sarah asked incredulously. "What is the message?"

"Good night, missy," Malinda said, turning to go on down the path. Sarah watched until she disappeared inside the blockhouse.

Something didn't feel right to Sarah. Why had Malinda been so eager to get her back inside the cabin? And if she knew what the drum was saying, why wouldn't she share it?

"What was that all about?" Ma questioned from behind her. "I heard you scream."

"Malinda nearly scared the wits out of me!" Sarah said. "That woman can sneak up on you just like an Indian! Then she started talking about witch doctors and voodoo drums and somebody sending a message."

"A message?" Ma repeated. "What kind of message?"

"I don't know, Ma."

"Well, come on back to bed, dear," Ma said. "At least one watchman seems to be wide awake and on guard. We might as well try to get some sleep. Who knows what we will face before it's over."

Still wearing her dress, Sarah lay down. For a long time, she lay listening to the silence, hearing the insects pick up their interrupted songs. Now and then the cry of a night bird made her wonder if that, too, were an Indian signal. The drum was silent, though, and sometime during the night, she finally fell asleep.

For two nights after that, there was no drummer to wake them in the middle of the night. Then just before she dozed off on the third night, Sarah heard the rhythmic boom-boom-boom begin again. She got up, went to the doorway, and stood listening.

Finally she went back to bed, for the drumming continued for hours. And that was just the beginning. As August slipped into September, the throbbing beat of a drum in the night became as commonplace as the chirping of crickets in the chimney corner. Sometimes when it woke her, Sarah, like the rest of her family, would just turn over and go back to sleep. Some nights she would get up and stand or sit in the doorway for a while, listening, watching, hoping for a breeze to cool the stuffy cabin.

One night as she sat in the doorway fanning herself with the hem of her nightgown, wishing for a fresh bucket of water from the spring, she saw a dark figure appear in the doorway of Colonel Clark's blockhouse.

Instinctively, Sarah stepped behind the door frame and peeked around it. The figure stood still a moment, and as her eyes adjusted, Sarah could see that it was Malinda. She was dressed in dark colors and carried something under one arm. She cast a glance all around, then slipped past the corner of the blockhouse and disappeared into the shadows.

Was Malinda going to the spring? Sarah thought about

how good a drink of ice-cold water would taste, how good it would feel to splash some across her sweaty face. Should she get a bucket and follow Malinda to the spring?

Suddenly, Sarah heard a new sound, a faint squeaking noise. A horse whinnied softly from the corral beyond the back gates. Had someone gone out to check on the horses? No one was supposed to open the gates for any reason without permission, and never at night, unless the guards were convinced some settler was out there seeking refuge.

Again, a horse whinnied, then blew air through its nostrils. There was no doubt the horses were disturbed about something.

"Who goes there?" a sentry cried, and Sarah heard him cock his gun. She wondered if Malinda were out there somewhere, creeping among the shadows.

Then Sarah saw Malinda slip back inside the Reynolds' blockhouse, this time obviously carrying a bucket by the handle. The bucket was wet and appeared to be heavy, for Malinda leaned slightly from its weight.

Sarah saw two men run from the northeast blockhouse down toward the spring. Another man ran past Sarah, then cut across the compound toward the corral gates. She could hear them talking in low voices. The gates creaked open, then in a few moments slammed shut again. She heard the holding bar scrape into place, realizing that was the sound she had heard earlier.

"I know somebody was in that corral," one of the men said, as they came back up the path toward her.

"Well, there's no one there now," another answered.

"That holding bar wasn't all the way down in the slot," the third said worriedly. "And I know I checked it before dark."

"You're imagining things, Jake," the second man assured him. "You both are. Nobody opened those gates and went into the corral. We've watched those gates like hawks!"

"Still, I'd feel better if we conducted a cabin search," the third speaker insisted, poking his head inside the cabin next to the Moores' cabin. The others went into the blockhouse where Malinda had disappeared.

Sarah jumped into bed and pretended to be asleep. She could feel the men's eyes searching the cabin; then they moved on down the row, leaving her wide awake and wondering what Malinda had been up to. Why had she opened the stockade gates in the middle of the night, with Indians out there just waiting for the chance to get inside?

Maybe I should wake Pa and tell him, but Malinda has been so good to us! Sarah thought as she lay still listening to Jamie's soft breathing beside her. Why, Ma and little Elizabeth might not be alive if Malinda hadn't taken such good care of them! Could Sarah just callously turn her in for . . . for what?

Sarah sighed. Maybe she could just keep an eye on her for a while. Maybe, as Malinda said, there was no threat from the drum. At least it was silent now, she thought gratefully, feeling herself growing sleepy.

When Sarah next opened her eyes, Ma was up making biscuits. "Thank goodness those drums have stopped! My head just throbs with them," she said, cutting out another circle of dough and placing it with the others in the greased spider. She put the top on the three-legged skillet and set it in the coals of the fireplace to bake. "I've never felt so threatened in my life," she said.

"Sticks and stones may break your bones, but tom-toms will never hurt you," Pa teased. Ma gave him a dirty look.

"Malinda says the drum is not threatening," Sarah put in, adding a little salt to the bowl of eggs she was preparing for scrambling. "She says somebody is just sending messages."

"What does Malinda know about it?" Luke scoffed, coming into the cabin after a night of guard duty. Sarah was surprised to see a faint stubble of beard on his jaw. Her brother was growing up!

"Just knowing the Indians are out there in the woods is threat enough for me," Luke went on. "How many do you think there are, Pa? And why can't our scouts locate them?"

"I don't know, son," Pa answered. "You'd think they would leave some trace, but there's not even a mashed-down patch of grass to show where they've been!"

"They're out there somewhere, though," Luke said.

Pa nodded. "I know. I want to get started rebuilding our cabin, but I've been afraid to leave the fort with Indian attack likely."

Suddenly, Sarah remembered her gifts. "Pa," she cried, running to the deerskin bag and pulling out the package of hinges and nails, "I brought you something from Williamsburg!"

Pa reached for the parcel. "What on earth?" he asked, as his hand dropped under its weight.

Sarah handed Luke the parcel that now held only a handful of nonpareils. "I brought these for you, Luke," she apologized, "but I'm afraid Jamie and Ruthie have about done for them!" Then she cautioned, "Don't open it in front of you-know-who!"

"What is it?" Luke questioned, peeking inside.

"It's c-a-n-d-y," she spelled, throwing a glance at the trundle bed where Jamie still lay sleeping.

"Why, Sary girl!" Pa exclaimed. "These hinges and nails are just what I need for our new front door! No leather greased with bear fat for us this time!" He laid the package on the table and came over to give her a quick hug. "What a thoughty gift!" he said. "I thank you kindly."

Embarrassed, Sarah beat the egg mixture furiously, making it foam. Then she poured it into the hot skillet.

"Something's been puzzling me," Pa said, going back to

the topic they had been discussing before Sarah's gifts. "I've never heard Indian tom-toms like these. There's something different about the sound, the rhythm. I can't put my finger on it though."

Sarah stirred the eggs with a long wooden spoon to keep them from sticking. Should she tell Pa about Malinda going out to the corral? But what was there to tell? Had Malinda really done anything wrong?

Jamie got up and came over to stand by the table, watching solemnly with wide blue eyes. Finally, he dropped his gaze to the floor, and Sarah heard him whisper, "Roofie?"

"We'll go see Ruthie after 'while," she snapped, discouraged that even having the family all back together hadn't helped him recall their old closeness. Then, as Jamie's lip began to tremble, she said quickly, "I'm sorry, sweets. Eat your breakfast and then we'll go see Ruthie."

"The Carsons' dog had pups," Luke announced around a mouthful of hot biscuit and gravy. "I think Hunter is their pa. One of them looks just like him."

Suddenly, Sarah had an inspiration. "Eat your breakfast, Jamie, and I'll take you to see the puppies," she promised.

"Puppies?" Jamie echoed doubtfully. But he began to eat.

As soon as breakfast was over and she had helped wash and dry the dishes, Sarah led Jamie out the door and up the path to the Carsons' cabin. They found the old mother dog lying in the outside chimney corner with her litter of seven squirming puppies tumbling over her and each other.

A grin spread across Jamie's face as he squatted down to watch. Then one little brown and black pup ran over and licked him in the face. Jamie laughed aloud.

"He likes you, Jamie!" Sarah said.

Jamie nodded, his eyes on the frisking pup.

"Young man, would you like to have one of those puppies?" Mrs. Carson asked from the cabin doorway.

Jamie looked up at her eagerly, then back at the pup. Finally, he looked up at Sarah. "Can I, Sadie?" he begged. "Can I have the puppy?"

Sarah's heart turned over. Jamie had used his old name for her, something he hadn't done since she had come home. She wanted to agree right now with his plaintive request but replied, "We'll have to ask Ma, but I suspect she'll let you have it."

Jamie ran back to where the pup was busily getting his breakfast. He reached down to pat it on the brown spot on its neck.

"Is that the one you want, honey," Mrs. Carson asked, "that frisky little brown spotted one?"

Jamie nodded, his eyes and his hands still on the pup.

"They're too young to leave their ma yet," Mrs. Carson said to Sarah, "but as soon as that one's weaned he can have it, provided your ma says so. And you can come play with it anytime you want to," she told Jamie.

"Come on, Jamie," Sarah urged, "let's go ask Ma if you can have him."

He took her hand and let her lead him away, all the while looking back over his shoulder at the pup.

When Ma had agreed to the addition to their family, Sarah walked with Jamie over to the Larkins' cabin as she had promised earlier.

"Roofie! Roofie!" he called as they came through the doorway, "I'm gonna get a puppy! He's got brown spots and he likes me!"

★ Chapter Eleven ★

Ruthie looked up from the corncob farm. "Can I have one, too?" she asked. "Puppies like me, too."

"I don't know," Jamie said. "I didn't ask for you. But you can ask the lady. Can't she, Sadie?" he asked, looking up at his sister.

Betsy looked up at Sarah and smiled. "Looks like you're his big sister again," she whispered.

Sarah nodded happily. It felt so good to have him look at her with recognition in his eyes, to hear him call her by his old baby name for her. "I'll be back for him," she said to Betsy, "if it's all right for him to play here for a while." She hoped Jamie's newfound acceptance of her would not be forgotten when she returned.

Sarah spent the morning helping Ma with Elizabeth and with chores around the cabin, and the afternoon tutoring the Reynolds girls.

Just before supper, she went to get Jamie.

"Can we go see my puppy, Sadie?" he asked, reaching up to take her hand, his reluctance to leave the Larkins apparently forgotten. And, after they had visited "Spot," Jamie let her take him home, feed him his supper, and put him to bed. Soon he was fast asleep.

When Sarah went to bed, she lay awake awhile, waiting for the drum to start. When it did, she got up, put on her dress and moccasins, and stood in the doorway until she saw Malinda creep out of the blockhouse and down toward the gates, carrying her bucket.

Quickly Sarah followed, keeping close to the cabins so Malinda wouldn't see her if the moon came out from behind the clouds. She hid behind the big iron kettle the women used to wash clothes down by the spring, watching Malinda struggle to open the heavy bar silently. Either

Malinda had greased the bar or she had learned to move it without noise. She slipped through the gate and pushed it to behind her.

Sarah ran to the gate and slipped through, finding herself in the corral. The horses shied away from her, but she located Gracie and took hold of her soft nose. The little brown mare made a low, rumbling sound of greeting deep in her throat, but she stood calmly, letting Sarah stroke her. The other horses seemed to interpret the mare's acceptance of her to mean she was no threat to them.

Sarah was grateful that Gracie remembered her, for she hadn't had an opportunity to ride her since they came to Harrodstown, and she was cared for by the men with the rest of the horses. Sarah wrapped some of the mare's mane around her hand and, walking beside her, urged her to move slowly across the pen, praying none of the horses would whinny. At the fence, she let go of Gracie's mane and crawled between the wooden poles that formed the corral. She stood there looking around. Where had Malinda gone?

Just then, the clouds moved away from the moon, and she saw Malinda going into the woods, carrying her bucket. Sarah hesitated, looking at the unprotected expanse of open meadow, gleaming silver in the moonlight. Anybody crossing it would be a target for flying arrows, or bullets from the settlers' guns! She was amazed that a guard hadn't seen Malinda and sounded the alarm.

Soon Malinda reappeared at the edge of the forest. She stood waiting until the moon went behind the clouds. Then Sarah could barely see her, moving across the meadow. When the clouds moved, Malinda quickly dropped flat on her stomach in the tall meadow grass.

So that was how she did it!

Sarah climbed back inside the corral and walked Gracie back to the gates, whispering in her ear and rubbing her velvety nose. She slipped through the unbarred gate and down to the spring. There, she hid behind the big iron kettle again.

Sarah peered around the kettle and saw Malinda come through the gate and reach up to fasten the bar. Then she came to the spring and dipped her bucket into the water. She rinsed it out, then filled it and turned to carry it up the path.

"Malinda!" Sarah hissed, stepping out from behind the kettle.

Malinda jumped and spilled water into her moccasins. "You startled me, missy!" she whispered angrily, turning to face Sarah. "Why are you out here sneaking up on folks when they go after fresh water?"

"What were you doing out in the woods, Malinda?" Sarah shot back. "Aren't you afraid of the Indians? Or have you become such good friends with them that you no longer fear them?"

"You be spying on Malinda!" the big woman accused indignantly.

"Don't change the subject, Malinda!" Sarah whispered back. "I felt I owed you a chance to explain your activities before I told Pa about them."

Malinda stared at her, her dark eyes unreadable in the moonlight. "You don't want to be doing that, missy," she said finally. "I warn you, don't be telling anybody anything about Malinda!" With that, she turned and walked toward the blockhouse with her bucket of water.

Sarah could hardly believe it! Malinda had threatened her!

"Halt right there!" Sarah heard a man's voice order. "What are you doing out here?"

"Malinda just be coming back from the spring with a bucket of water, sir," Sarah heard the woman answer softly. "Is something wrong?"

"It's after midnight!" the man said. "Do you often prowl around this time of night?"

"Malinda couldn't sleep, sir," she explained, "with the heat and . . . "

" . . . the drums," he finished for her. They've got everybody's nerves on edge. But somebody's been opening the gates and going into the corral with the horses. That wasn't you, was it?"

"Sir, Malinda be going after a fresh bucket of cold water this hot night," she answered evasively. "Malinda has nothing to do with horses!"

"All right," the sentry finally agreed. "Get on with your bucket of water. And stay inside till morning. Everybody's jumpy, and you could be mistaken for an intruder and shot."

"Yes, sir. Malinda be going to bed now. Thank you, sir," she said.

Sarah could hear them moving away from her. Cautiously, she edged along the wall and slipped inside her cabin. She took off her dress and moccasins, slipped on her nightgown, and lay down on the trundle bed beside Jamie.

"Sadie?" he muttered drowsily. Then he turned over on his stomach, pushed both arms up under his pillow, and soon was breathing deeply and regularly. Sarah knew he was asleep.

She lay awake, thinking about the evening's events. Malinda was the one opening the gates. Still, Malinda hadn't exactly lied to the guard. She had gone to get a bucket of water, but she had evaded his question about the gates.

What was Malinda doing? Was she plotting with the Indians against the settlers? If so, why? She seemed very fond of Anabelle Reynolds and her daughters. She seemed to care about Ma and Elizabeth; she certainly had worked tirelessly to help them both get well and strong. And she had received nothing in return.

It was a mystery, Sarah thought yawning, and one she would not be able to solve that night. Nor did it seem any clearer in the morning, though word of Malinda's nighttime wanderings had spread.

I knew it the minute I laid eyes on her!" Mrs. Butler commented as Sarah took her place behind three ladies who had come to the spring before her.

"I don't know," Mrs. Larkin put in, "she healed Mark's leg that was poisoned by that arrow. Put some kind of poultice on it, and it healed right up. And it's a miracle what she's done for Della Moore and that poor little sickly baby!"

"That only goes to prove it!" Mrs. Butler insisted. "She has special powers!"

"Are you saying Malinda's a witch?" Mrs. Carson asked.

"Well, Mrs. Thurman got after her one day for helping herself to some herbs from her chimney corner. After that, the Thurmans' cow gave onion-flavored milk for a week, and their little boy's hand broke out in warts all over," Mrs. Butler said.

Mrs. Larkin laughed. "Everybody's cows gave onion-flavored milk after they got into that patch of wild onions."

"Everybody's young 'uns didn't sprout warts!" Mrs. Butler pointed out.

"I don't know about all that," Mrs. Carson put in, "but I've never seen a slave so uppity. And Anabelle Reynolds lets her get by with it. It's just not fitting!"

"What are they going to do with Malinda?" Mrs. Larkin asked. Sarah supposed Mrs. Larkin had mixed feelings about Malinda too, since she owed her a debt of gratitude for Mr. Larkin's healing.

"My Gabe was on guard duty last night," Mrs. Carson said. "He caught her prowling around the compound, but he says they've got nothing against her except suspicions. He questioned her and had to let her go. But, mark my words, that woman's as guilty as sin!"

"What's she guilty of?" Mrs. Larkin asked.

Mrs. Carson turned to stare at her. "She's helping the Indians!" she replied indignantly. "We'll wake up one of these mornings with the place crawling with 'em, and there won't be a thing we can do!"

"But why would she want to help the Indians?" Mrs. Larkin pursued. Sarah had wondered that, too. What could Malinda gain from helping them take the fort? Wouldn't they just scalp her, too?

"Who knows why slaves do what they do," Mrs. Butler mused. "But there's many a story of uprisings where whole families were wiped out by their slaves. Why, back in Georgia, our neighbors down the road woke up one night to find their whole plantation on fire and their livestock slaughtered. They barely escaped into the swamp with their lives," she said, taking the place Mrs. Carson vacated after filling her bucket with water. "To be honest, you could hardly blame the poor slaves, if you knew how they were treated, but still and all . . . "

"I don't see why Malinda would want to harm Anabelle Reynolds," Mrs. Larkin interrupted. "She seems very fond of her, and I've never so much as heard Mrs. Reynolds raise her voice to her."

"Maybe the Indians have promised her freedom," Mrs. Carson suggested. "A slave will do anything for that!"

"Who knows why slaves do what they do," Mrs. Butler repeated, swinging her filled bucket out of the way to make room for Mrs. Larkin's.

Mrs. Larkin filled her bucket and turned around. "Why, Sarah, I didn't know you were back there! How's Jamie taking to being home again?"

"He's doing fine, Mrs. Larkin," Sarah assured her, "especially now that he's got that puppy to think about. And I'm so glad to have him home, but we surely do appreciate all you and Betsy have done for him. I don't know what Ma and I would have done without you!"

"Oh, pshaw, Sarah," Mrs. Larkin said, her face flushing with embarrassment. "It was no more than anybody would have done. And when I think of all your family did for us when we settled on Stoney Creek . . . well, it was the least we could do."

Sarah knelt to dip her bucket in the spring. When she stood, the women were gone and Malinda waited her turn at the water.

"You be talking with the ladies about Malinda?" she asked, studying Sarah through narrowed eyes.

"No, Malinda," Sarah answered truthfully. "I was just listening to them talk."

"And what they be saying?"

"Oh, just repeating rumors and what Pa calls 'old wives' tales,' " Sarah said.

Malinda smiled a slow, unamused smile. "Things like, 'That Malinda has the evil eye. She makes the cows give onion milk or a chile grow warts! She can heal or harm according to her wishes!' Things like that?"

Sarah nodded. "Old wives' tales," she said.

Malinda's dark eyes bore into hers. "Don't be too sure, missy," she warned. "Sometimes old wives' tales be more truth than folks think."

"Well, then, are you a witch, Malinda?" Sarah asked boldly. "Is there truth in that?"

Malinda laughed. "Let them believe what they will," she said with an indifferent shrug of her broad shoulders.

"But you do have special powers, Malinda. You made Ma and Elizabeth well, and you healed Mark Larkin's leg," Sarah continued. "How do you explain all that, if it wasn't magic or witchcraft?"

Malinda shook her head violently. "No, missy, don't even say it! Malinda has seen the witch doctors in Barbados make what they call 'the magic.' They perform terrible deeds in the name of their dark god, Diabolos. Malinda be wanting no part of that!"

"Diabolos?" Sarah repeated.

"The one you call the Devil or Satan," Malinda explained. "Believe me, they be evil ones and their magic be evil."

"But maybe your magic is a good magic, Malinda," Sarah insisted. "Maybe it's not something dark and evil. Maybe it's . . . "

"All magic is evil, Miss Sarah," she interrupted. "All magic comes from the Evil One, the Diabolos."

"Then how do you do the wonderful things you do?"

116

"Malinda has learned how to use the things God caused to grow on this earth to help heal folks," the woman said. "There's nothing magic about it. Malinda just be using prayer and common sense, that's all."

Sarah thought about that a moment, then a new thought hit her. "But you understand the language of the drums," she reminded her. "You told me you did."

Malinda nodded. "Understanding and being a part of be two different things, young miss," she said.

Then Sarah remembered another question she had pondered. "Is the language of the Indian drums the same as the language of the drums of Barbados?"

"They be different," Malinda admitted warily.

"But you said there was no threat from this drummer, that he was only sending messages," Sarah persisted. "How do you know that if the language of the Indian tom-toms is different?"

Malinda stared at her out of those unreadable dark eyes. "That drum not be played by an Indian," she said finally.

"Don't be ridiculous, Malinda," Sarah scoffed. "Of course it's an Indian! What else could it be?"

But Malinda was shaking her head, again. "This drummer be no Indian," she insisted, lifting her bucket of water and heading up the slope toward the blockhouse.

Sarah picked up her bucket and walked toward the cabin. What could Malinda mean? She vowed to question her further when she went to give the Reynolds girls their afternoon lessons.

Malinda, though, was nowhere in sight when Sarah entered the blockhouse that afternoon. Mrs. Reynolds was rocking the baby, and the girls sat around the table, making patchwork doll quilts from scraps of material.

"You're as crazy as old Dulcie, Caroline!" little Lucy was saying as Sarah came into the big room. "Next thing we know, you'll be rocking back and forth, making that awful sound she used to make!"

Dulcie? Was that the name Lucy had used?

"Lucy!" Mrs. Reynolds scolded. "Shame on you for making fun of the afflicted! Don't ever let me hear you do that again!"

"But, Ma, it was an awful sound," Caroline said in Lucy's defense. "It just grated on my nerves!"

"And she was crazy, Ma," Felicity backed up her sisters.

"I suppose she was, girls," their mother said, "but that poor woman had endured horrible things, and her mind finally just snapped. She was to be pitied, not ridiculed."

"I'm sorry, Ma," Lucy murmured, her big blue eyes bordering on tears.

"Did you say Dulcie?" Sarah asked the little girl.

Lucy threw a questioning glance at her mother, then dropped her gaze to the material she held in her hand, apparently afraid to say anything more.

Sarah turned to Mrs. Reynolds. "Did she say Dulcie, ma'am?" she repeated.

"She was a slave who was captured by the Indians, Sarah, after they massacred her owners," Mrs. Reynolds explained. "Eventually she escaped and made her way to the fort at Boonesborough, but her mind just wasn't right. Only God knows what the poor woman had endured!" She shuddered.

"She wouldn't talk," Caroline said. "She just sat in a chair and rocked back and forth, staring at the wall and humming an off-key tune."

"It wasn't a tune, really," Felicity corrected. "It was

more like the wailing of some wounded animal!" She shuddered. "It was awful!"

"What happened to her? After that, I mean," Sarah questioned eagerly. Could this be Marcus's Dulcie? Was she on the verge of finding her at last?

"Oh, she ran away," Lucy answered matter-of-factly, sticking the end of her tongue out of the corner of her mouth and chewing on it with the effort to cut around the corners of her quilt square.

"You're the one who's crazy, Lucy!" Caroline exclaimed. "Look at you, chewing on your own tongue! Do you think that will help you cut straighter?"

"Honey, that square just isn't going to work. Throw it away, and I'll help you cut a new one," Felicity offered.

"Where did she go?" Sarah persisted. "After she left the fort, was she ever heard from again?"

"I don't know, dear," Mrs. Reynolds answered. "We left Boonesborough soon after that. I really don't know what happened to her. They said she was searching for her lost son. I suppose he was still with the Indians." She laid the baby on the bed. "Time for lessons, girls!" she said. "Put away your sewing now. We'll practice another time."

Sarah felt frustration mounting inside her. This had to be Marcus's Dulcie! She seemed so close to finding her. She knew Dulcie had been at Boonesborough. What she needed to know now was where she had gone after that.

"Tell us about Williamsburg, Sarah," Caroline begged. "Wouldn't it be wonderful to go there and shop in the stores, Ma?"

Mrs. Reynolds sighed. "Honey, I haven't been inside a store for so long, I hardly remember what it was like! I surely could use some new buttons and a piece or two of ribbon."

★ Reunion in Kentucky ★

"They'd have lemon-scented soap," Caroline went on, closing her eyes to help her recall the smell. "I hate the scent of that old lye soap!"

"And the store would smell like vanilla and cinnamon under the lemon," Felicity remembered.

"I don't 'member much about it," Lucy admitted.

"You don't even remember the candies or the doll's tea sets?" Caroline asked.

Mrs. Reynolds gave Lucy a hug. "I guess you don't remember Charleston at all," she said sadly. "You were so little when we left. We had a lovely little brick house on the Common, and inside it was furnished with beautiful pieces from England and France."

"There were rich draperies at the windows and thick carpets on the floors," Felicity recalled, casting a scornful glance at the wooden window shutter and the rough log floor.

"And in the evenings after supper, sometimes we would stroll down to the waterfront to watch the boats come in, bringing more wonders from across the ocean," Caroline added. "It was a wonderful place! Sort of like Williamsburg, I guess, Sarah."

"I wish we'd never left it," their mother said. "Maybe then your father would still be alive." She made a soft choking sound and excused herself from the room.

"Girls, do you remember your conjugations?" Sarah changed the subject hastily.

As the girls recited their lessons, though, Sarah found her thoughts going back to the crazy woman the Reynolds had encountered at Boonesborough. How awful it would be to rescue her, only to find that they must take Marcus a crazy woman instead of the graceful wife he remembered who could sing like a nightingale!

Would it be better to "leave it be," as Malinda had advised?

"But I can't!" Sarah said aloud, as later she made her way home. "I have to find her, no matter what!" But how? Again, it seemed that Boonesborough held the key to Dulcie's whereabouts, and she made up her mind to ask Pa to take her there right away.

Pa, though, wasn't at the cabin when she got home.

"He has sentry duty tonight," Ma explained, ladling stew into bowls and setting them on the table. "He'll be in the blockhouse most of the night, I reckon. I just took him some supper."

Sarah sighed. Her request would have to wait until morning or likely tomorrow afternoon, for Pa would come in tired and wanting to sleep. But she vowed she would ask him to take her to Boonesborough at the earliest opportunity. She had to find Dulcie!

Here they come!" a sentry called early the next morning.

"God help us!" another man shouted. "There's hundreds of 'em!"

"I told you they'd be back!" a third man reminded them.

Any further words were lost in the sound of gunfire that went on without ceasing for hours. Sarah's head throbbed with the sound as she carried little Elizabeth around to keep her calm.

"Hand me the baby, Sarah, and go set one of the buckets of water outside in the chimney corner," Ma said, pouring melted lead into Pa's bullet molds. "If a burning arrow lands on that roof, we'll need water in a hurry!"

"Bang! Bang!" Jamie shouted, racing around the cabin, pointing his finger at Ma, then at Sarah.

"Jamie! Stop it!" Sarah ordered, handing Ma the baby. "It's bad enough out there, without you carrying on so!"

"Sadie's right, Jamie," Ma said, setting the bullets aside to harden. "We don't need to add to the noise."

Jamie stood looking at the floor, his lower lip in a pout.

"Here, sweets, you can look at the pictures in *The Pilgrim's Progress*, if you will be very careful not to soil the pages," Sarah offered, feeling guilty for yelling at him. She handed him the little leather volume.

Jamie looked up at her, his blue eyes widening in surprise. Sarah never let him touch her book! She smiled at him encouragingly, swallowing her fears for her most treasured possession. When he took the book from her, she reached for one of the water buckets she had filled this morning.

"Make another batch when those are dry, Della," Pa said, coming into the cabin and eyeing the filled bullet molds. He scooped up a handful of already dried bullets from the mantel.

"How many Indians are out there?" Ma asked.

"It's hard to tell. Hundreds, I reckon," Pa answered. "And there's a handful of Frenchmen with them. Our scout says they're at Boonesborough, too, so there's no use sending over there for help."

"Where do they get so many?" Ma asked. "Can we hold them off, Hiram?"

"Pray that we can!" he answered, running back out the door and toward the front of the fort.

Sarah stood with the bucket of water in her hand, watching him climb a ladder to the walkway around the top of the log wall, where the men stood shooting down on the Indians as they charged across the clearing toward the fort. She said a quick prayer for his safety.

Then she added a prayer for Luke, wherever he was.

★ Chapter Thirteen ★

She couldn't see him anywhere, so she decided he must be inside one of the blockhouses. From there he could shoot through one of the little square loopholes, or load guns for others as they shot.

I could do that, she thought enviously. Pa had taught her long ago how to load and fire a gun. There was no telling when she and Ma might have to defend themselves when he and Luke were away on various tasks.

"We'll need to fix some nourishing food," Ma broke into her thoughts. "The men will be tired and hungry."

Well, so much for helping fight Indians! Sarah thought with disappointment. It was always the same old story—prepare food, wash up, help with the young ones. But she reckoned that was the way it was for womenfolk.

Just then, she saw Betsy Larkin leave her cabin and head for the corner blockhouse, carrying a powder horn and a leather pouch.

"What are you doing, Betsy?" she called, "taking ammunition to your pa?"

"No, I'm loading the gun for Luke while he shoots!" she called back. "Can't stop to talk now! He's near out of bullets!"

"See you later!" Sarah called. She sighed, then turned to go back inside the cabin to help Ma prepare vegetables for the kettle. It seemed that everybody had something important to do, while, as usual, she was stuck peeling potatoes or stringing beans. She stabbed a potato viciously with the paring knife.

Ma threw her a questioning glance. "The men have to be fed, Sarah, to keep up their strength. If we're all off loading guns, who will prepare the food?"

"I don't know, Ma," she muttered.

★ Reunion in Kentucky ★

"Oh, honey, I understand," Ma said sympathetically. "It's always the men who get to do the exciting, heroic deeds, while we women are left with the drudgery. But maybe that's because our Maker has given us a special endurance. Maybe He knew most men would lose interest and go off hunting or fishing if they had to do the dull, unending chores like cooking and cleaning and caring for a crying baby all day long."

"It just doesn't seem fair, Ma," Sarah said, dropping the peeled potato into the pot of water Ma had ready over the fire. "We're always so tied down! And they're always so free!"

Ma smiled. "No matter what our hands are busy doing, honey, our minds can soar above it all," she said. "Why, I don't know how many thousand pounds of potatoes I've peeled in my time, and, you know, I don't remember more than half a dozen of them! All that time, hours of it, my mind was as free as an eagle flying over mountains! And some of my best dreaming has been done with a needle or a scrub brush in my hand!"

"I reckon you're right, Ma," Sarah agreed. "I never thought about it that way. But I think I could load a gun or two and still have time for all that."

Ma chuckled. "I'll feed Elizabeth, and you fix Jamie something," was all she said, but she reached over to pat Sarah's hand as though she understood, and maybe even agreed.

Suddenly, Sarah noticed that the shooting had stopped. There was no howling or screeching, either. Soon after that, Pa and Luke came into the cabin.

"Whoever invented loopholes so we could shoot out and arrows can't come in was a genius!" Luke said, taking

126

his place at the table. "The blockhouse is the place to be with Indians all around."

"I like the freedom of raising up over those logs and aiming that gun wherever I want to, without the restrictions the loopholes impose," Pa answered. "But inside that blockhouse is exactly where I want you to be, son, even if you are one of the finest marksmen in this fort!" Sarah saw Luke puff up a little at Pa's rare praise.

"Are the Indians gone?" she asked, setting a bowl of steaming stew on the table in front of Pa.

Pa shook his head. "No, Sary, I'm afraid not. They've retired into the woods for now, but they'll be back, and when we least expect 'em! That's why we're eating and keeping watch in shifts."

Sarah set a bowl of stew in front of Luke. "Could I help load the guns, Pa?" she asked. "If Ma doesn't need me?"

Pa looked at her, then at Ma. "Why, Sary girl, I don't know. . . ."

"Betsy's been loading for Luke today," she interrupted. "I could load for you. I know how, and I would do exactly what you told me."

"It's dangerous up there, Sary," he said. "The Indians won't be likely to climb the wall. We've got hot kettles of lye water to pour down on them from the blockhouse overhangs if they try. There's no telling when a flaming arrow may come sailing over that wall, though."

"I could use somebody to load for me in the block-house," Luke offered. "I don't think Betsy is coming back this afternoon."

"Please, Pa!" Sarah begged. "Just for a little while?"

Pa studied her for a moment, then he sighed. "All right, Sary," he said, "if your ma can spare you."

"Oh, Hiram, I don't think she should," Ma began. "What if she got hit by an arrow? You know, Mark Larkin's leg was poisoned for months, and . . . "

"Della, no place in this fort is safe right now," Pa interrupted. "Those Indians could come swarming over the roof of this cabin easier than they could the stockade walls. Some have tried, but, thank God, we've seen them in time to stop them!"

"Not one single arrow has ever made it through a loophole in one of our blockhouses!" Luke bragged, as though he, personally, had built all three of them.

"Come on, then, Sary girl," Pa said, getting up from the table and reaching for his gun, powder horn, and bullet pouch.

Suddenly the air was shredded by screeching and howling that seemed to fill the cabin and the space around it.

"They're back!" Luke shouted. "Let's go!"

"Oh, Lord, help us!" Ma breathed.

Sarah shivered with fear. Now that she had the chance, she wasn't sure she wanted to get any closer to the fighting. Maybe she wasn't as brave as she had thought. But she couldn't admit that now. Luke would never let her live it down. She threw Ma a frightened look, took a deep breath, and plunged out the door after Luke and Pa.

She saw Pa climbing the ladder to the walkway. Luke ran inside the blockhouse at the end of the row of cabins. Sarah followed him upstairs, slowly placing one foot after another on the narrow steps, waiting for her eyes to adjust to the dimness.

Then Luke was showing her where to stand and what to do, and she had no time to think of anything but pouring powder, ramming shot, handing the loaded gun to her brother, and taking the smoking, empty one from him to reload. Her ears rang with the loud explosions of the guns all around them. Her eyes, nostrils, and lungs burned with the acrid scent of gun powder that hung like a cloud in the air.

Outside, there were no melodious night bird sounds. Instead, the wild screeching of the Indians as wave after wave of them stormed the fort, then receded under the accurate and deadly gunfire of the settlers, reminded her of the shrill din of the locusts that had descended on the farm back in Virginia one summer.

Would the Indians, like the locusts, eventually exhaust themselves and go away? Or would they keep coming until they destroyed everything in their path, leaving the fort as bare and empty as the locusts had left the fruit trees back home? Many of those trees had not survived. Would there be any settlers left when this siege was over? Or, if they managed to survive this one, would they make it through the next one, or the next?

Then as suddenly as it had begun, the attack stopped. One by one, the men stopped shooting. The silence was so deep it hurt Sarah's ears.

"Take a breather, men, while you can," James Harrod advised. "Every other man rest and eat, while the others stand guard. Then switch off. The Indians will likely be back in a little while."

Sarah stretched her tired arms above her head. She had thought carrying water and wood and scrubbing floors was hard work, but after several hours of loading and reloading guns, her arms ached with weariness and her head throbbed with the memory of relentless noise.

Some of the women came into the blockhouse with

food and a bucket of cold water. Sarah took the cup they offered her and drank thirstily. She took two biscuits with meat on them and sank down on the floor, resting her tired back against the rough log wall.

"Jumping toadfrogs!" Luke exclaimed, his eye still at a loophole, keeping watch. "I didn't know Indians had slaves!"

"Why, young 'un, they'd make a slave out of you if they could capture you!" Gabe Carson said with a laugh. "They don't usually let captives fight, though. How do you know he's a slave?"

"He's not fighting," Luke answered. "He's carrying water to the braves. See? There, at the edge of the forest."

"The scoundrels!" Mr. Carson grumbled. "Sitting there as bold as brass, taunting us, knowing they're beyond the range of our guns!" He put his eye to a loophole. "Why, it's a black man! Hey, Mark, looky here! The Indians have got 'em a black slave."

Mark Larkin moved to the loophole. "There's a story over at Boonesborough about a slave woman and her son being captured by Indians on their way into Kentucky. Their owners were killed, I understand."

"The woman escaped," James Harrod put in, "and made her way back to the fort, but the boy never was seen again. It may be just as well. He's probably half savage himself by now."

Was that Marcus's long lost son out there? Sarah's heart began to pound as she peered out a loophole.

"That could be the boy out there, I reckon," Mr. Carson said. "He's too far away to tell if he's full grown."

"Here they come again!" Luke cried.

Wearily, Sarah got up and took her place behind her

★ Chapter Thirteen ★

brother, with her dwindling supply of powder and bullets, praying the attack would soon be over. She was eager now to find out if that were Samuel they had seen out there today.

How could she find out, though? If the Indians left, they likely would take Sam with them. And if they stayed, she couldn't venture outside the fort to seek him. Or Dulcie.

Oh, Marcus, she thought, *I'm sorry it's taking so long to find Dulcie and Sam. But I will!* she vowed, handing Luke the loaded gun and taking the empty one from him. *I will find them if it's the last thing I do!*

On the thirteenth day of the siege, as Sarah tried to keep the Reynolds girls' minds on the wonders of the capitals of the world instead of the nerve-racking noises around them, the Indians sent a runner carrying a white flag to the fort. Word of the message spread quickly: If the leaders of the fort would meet with their leaders in the middle of the clearing, they would negotiate.

"Why don't they just leave?" Caroline asked, the strain of the past days showing plainly in her pale face and dark-circled eyes.

"What is there to negotiate, anyway?" Felicity added nervously. "Neither side has taken any prisoners. We certainly aren't going to agree to let the Indians inside the fort! And all we want from them is for them to leave!"

"Yeah!" Lucy echoed, freckles standing out across her nose with the intensity of her feelings. "You old Indians go away, and leave us alone!"

James Harrod, though, called a meeting of the settlers, and Sarah went with the girls to hear what he would say.

"I think the whole thing is a trick," he said frankly, dark eyes flashing angrily under a shock of dark hair. "The Indians want to lure us outside beyond gun range of the fort. Then they can capture us and use us as hostages to bargain with the ones left inside the fort."

"So we just ignore their little invitation?" Mark Larkin asked.

"No, we pretend to go along with it," Colonel Harrod answered. "Caleb, John, Hiram, and I go to meet with them. We stay just within range, with all the rest of you keeping your guns trained upon them, down low where they can't be seen. If there's trouble, I'll raise my arm in a signal, like this, and you fire immediately."

"What if they really do want to negotiate?" Caleb asked.

"Then we'll negotiate, whatever they mean by that," he said.

"Why should we bargain, Colonel?" Gabe Carson asked. "They haven't got a thing we want!"

"We're running very short on supplies—food, lead, powder. With the Indians camped all around us, obviously we can't go anywhere to replenish them. Thank God we have this good spring of water inside the fort, but that's about all we've got that won't run out in the next few days."

"We can't hunt, tend our crops, or even milk our cows," Pa added.

"I wish we'd had enough warning to get the cattle inside the fort," a woman muttered behind Sarah. "The Indians have probably already had 'em for supper!"

"I heard my Daisy bawling last night, so unless they've

had her for breakfast, she's still alive!" another woman said.

"If the siege goes on much longer," Colonel Harrod continued, "we'll really be hurting."

The settlers murmured agreement, and the Indian messenger was sent back with word that they would meet in the meadow. The men the colonel had named prepared to accompany him outside the gates.

"We'll have to leave our guns here," Colonel Harrod warned, tying a white rag to the end of a stick and handing it to Caleb. "But every one of you carry a hunting knife. Hide it where you can reach it in a hurry. Believe me, no matter how much they pretend otherwise, those Indians will be armed, and I don't aim for us to be totally defenseless out there!"

Sarah watched, her heart beating in her throat like a trapped bird, as one gate swung partly open and Pa walked through it with the others. The gate was shut and locked behind them.

"You're hurting my hand!" Lucy complained softly, and Sarah realized she was still holding the little girl's hand and was squeezing it in her anxiety for Pa.

She released Lucy, and saw her move over to stand beside Felicity, who put her arm around her. Mrs. Reynolds began to urge her children back toward their cabin.

Sarah threw a troubled glance at Ma standing beside her, holding Elizabeth in one arm and Jamie by the other hand. Ma had her eyes closed, her lips moving in silent prayer.

I can't stand not knowing what's happening to Pa! Sarah thought, running inside the blockhouse and upstairs to put her eye to a loophole. There they were, marching across that open field, with their white flag fluttering above them from the stick Caleb carried. They were nearly to the middle of the clearing. Were they still within firing range? And what were the Indians and their French associates planning as they marched to meet Pa and the others? What if the Indians fell upon the men and killed them all right before their eyes?

"Oh, Pa," she breathed, "be careful!"

Suddenly, Colonel Harrod's arm came up in the pre-arranged signal, and gunfire erupted from the fort. The four men began to run toward the gates, bent over to make smaller targets for flying arrows. The Indian "negotiators" ran back toward the trees, and a dozen or so armed braves ran boldly out into the meadow after Pa and the other men, some shooting arrows from their bows, others with tomahawks raised, all of them howling like wild dogs. They were almost on Pa and the others!

Then one of the men arched his back, stumbled, and fell. Sarah's heart turned over. It was Pa! And something was terribly wrong with him, for he just lay there like he was dead, with the Indians getting closer and closer! Sarah held her breath and closed her eyes, praying frantically. When she opened her eyes, James Harrod was running back to Pa. He picked him up and threw him over his shoulder, then ran on toward the fort, staggering under the added weight.

The Indians were dropping from the settlers' gunfire, but a few still ran after the men, zigzagging in a crouched run to avoid the bullets raining upon them from the fort.

"Hurry!" Sarah begged aloud. "They're gaining on you!"

Then the men were at the gates. The settlers eased one gate open enough for them to squeeze through, and slammed it shut right in the painted faces of two screeching braves. Sarah heard the bar slide into place. She saw that the other Indians had withdrawn beyond gun range, and the two nearest the fort had begun their zigzagging run back toward the trees. Just as quickly, she was running from the blockhouse toward her injured Pa.

Ma was there before her and had Pa's shirt open, examining the ugly wound across his back. Pa appeared to be unconscious, and Sarah shuddered at the sight of the blood that covered his back and had soaked through his shirt.

"Is he . . . will he? . . ." she stammered, afraid to voice her worst fears.

"He's alive," Colonel Harrod assured her, "but I don't know how bad he's hurt."

Sarah realized that he was holding Elizabeth for Ma, and reached to take her from him. "Thank you, sir, for going back after him," she said fervently, tears welling in her eyes.

He looked at her, then reached over and patted her hand. "There was no question of that, little girl," he said seriously. Then he turned and walked toward his block-house.

Betsy ran up and took Jamie in her arms. "Let's go play with Ruthie," she said, throwing Sarah a sympathetic glance.

Mark Larkin and Gabe Carson were carrying Pa toward the cabin, with Ma hurrying ahead to prepare a place for him. She turned to Sarah. "Go get Malinda!" she ordered. "Hurry!"

Sarah turned toward the far blockhouse and ran right into the big woman. Malinda looked at her for a moment out of those unreadable dark eyes, then followed Ma and the men into the cabin.

Sarah edged inside the doorway, trying to stay out of the way, but wanting to see how badly Pa was hurt.

"He be losing a lot of blood," Malinda said to Ma as they worked together to get Pa's shirt off and turn him on his stomach. "But it's God's blessing that tomahawk just sliced across his back and didn't bury itself in his body!" she said as she cleansed the wound, put some foul-smelling ointment on it, and began to wrap a clean cloth around Pa's back and chest.

Elizabeth started to cry, and Sarah carried her out to the stoop. She was grateful that Betsy had taken Jamie with her.

"He be all right, Miss Della," Sarah heard Malinda say to Ma. "Give him these powders in a cup of water, and when he wakes up, give him some meat, liver if you can get any. Make him drink lots of water. If the wound bleeds through the bandage tonight, replace it. Malinda be dressing it again tomorrow."

"Thank you, Malinda," Ma said, reaching out to take the woman's hand in both of hers. "I just don't know what we'd do without you!"

Malinda ducked her head. "It be nothing," she muttered. Then, as she left the cabin, "Malinda be back in the morning," she promised, giving Sarah a half smile as she passed.

"Thank you, Malinda," Sarah echoed Ma's words, rocking Elizabeth back and forth in her arms in a vain attempt to stop her crying.

Malinda placed her big hand on the baby's back and bent to whisper in her ear. Elizabeth stopped crying, and began to coo.

Pa groaned in pain, and Sarah turned to see Ma mixing the sleeping powders in a cup. "You men raise him up, if you can without hurting his back," she ordered. Pa cried out, but he swallowed the mixture, then sank back on his side and closed his eyes.

I can't stand to watch him suffer! Sarah thought, carrying Elizabeth rapidly away from the cabin. She walked over to the animal pens at the center of the compound and sank down on a bench under the sweet gum tree.

A huge red sun was sinking behind the western wall of the fort. It would be dark soon. Already the hot September day was beginning to cool a little, and a breeze gently ruffled the leaves above them. It was peaceful for the first time in thirteen days, and Sarah gratefully listened to the quiet murmur of voices down the row of cabins, as the settlers ate their suppers and prepared for bed.

Apparently, the Indians had gone. The men were on guard all around the fort, but there had been no further sign of them since Pa and the men had come back inside. Had they given up and gone back to their villages? Or were they still out there somewhere, waiting to launch the next attack? This was the longest it had been quiet since the attack started, so maybe they were gone. Sarah wished she knew!

A firefly flickered its light in front of them, and Elizabeth reached for it with one of her cooing sounds, but the little insect soared off above their heads.

Sarah remembered how her little cousin, Megan, had loved catching fireflies on the Palace Green back in Williamsburg. What would the perky little girl be up to about now? Would she be skipping down Nicholson Street to meet her sisters as they returned from shopping or from

visiting the new tutor? Would she be begging 'Gail or Tabby to go with her to catch fireflies? Or would she be out in the backyard under the big pine tree, playing with the tiger-striped kitten Sarah had talked Aunt Charity into letting her have? She missed Meggie dreadfully, she realized, hugging Elizabeth to her.

Elizabeth looked up at her and cooed, "Ah oooo!"

Sarah kissed the baby on her tiny nose. "I love you, too, Elizabeth," she said, pretending the baby knew what she was trying to say. Elizabeth was becoming precious to her, just as Jamie had been at her age, but she was just a baby. Megan was big enough to share things.

Sarah remembered how, almost every evening, she had spent some time with Meggie. Sometimes they simply had played hide-and-seek in the barn and stable, or run-sheep-run in the meadows behind the brick house. Sometimes they had gone to the palace gardens to throw bread crumbs to the geese and swans. Sometimes they had watched the militia drill on the Palace Green, Megan doing her best to whistle like the fifes and keep time to the drums with swaying head and tapping feet.

Suddenly, Sarah became aware that the drumming had started again. Her heart sank, knowing it wasn't the Williamsburg militia in their neat red and buff uniforms, but fierce Indians out there in the forest, seeking the death of everyone at Harrodstown.

But Malinda had said the drummer wasn't Indian. Then Sarah realized there was something different about the drumming this time. The rhythm was the same as before, but the soft boom-boom-boom seemed closer, and more toward the front of the stockade.

She caught her breath as three men left Harrod's blockhouse, their guns in their hands. They crept toward the front gates, and she heard the bar creak slightly as they opened one gate and slipped through it.

Sarah strained her ears to hear above the beat of the drum. Then a terrible commotion broke out near the graveyard. There was shouting from the men, but no shots were fired. Then there was a blood-curdling scream, followed by total silence.

Sarah eased over to the blockhouse and stood in the doorway, a sleepy Elizabeth nodding against her shoulder as she took in the scene inside. She had seen the men drag something or someone into the blockhouse, and she was determined to find out what was happening.

A thin woman sat on a ladder-back chair, her feet, in dirty Indian moccasins, barely touching the floor. Her hands, scratched and bleeding, were tied behind the chair with a rawhide thong. Her legs and arms were marked with new cuts and old scars, and there was a jagged tear in the skirt of her stained rawhide dress. Pieces of leaves and twigs clung to her thick, curly, white hair.

Was this Marcus's long-lost Dulcie? Sarah's heart began to pound against her chest, and her mouth was so dry her tongue stuck to it.

"Who are you?" Caleb questioned the captive.

Sarah held her breath to hear the answer, but the

woman stared at the floor, giving no indication that she had heard or understood the question.

"Let's get one of the women to question her," Mark Larkin suggested. "She's too scared to talk to us."

The woman looked up at the wall in front of her and smiled a slow, vacant smile. Then she began to rock back and forth, making the legs of the chair thump against the wooden floor.

"I'll get Emma," Gabe Carson offered, leaving the blockhouse.

In a few moments, Mrs. Carson came in and stood in front of the captive. "Who are you, woman?" she demanded, and Sarah wondered if it wouldn't have been better to get the gentle Mrs. Larkin to do the questioning.

The silent woman kept her gaze on the floor, rocking back and forth in the chair without rockers.

Mrs. Carson took hold of the woman's upper arms. "Look at me!" she said. "I asked you who you are!"

The captive continued to rock and began to hum, a high-pitched, tuneless sound that grated on Sarah's nerves.

"Stop that!" Mrs. Carson ordered, shaking her a little.

The woman stopped humming, but she continued to rock, staring blankly at the wall in front of her.

Mrs. Carson's face reddened angrily. For a moment, Sarah was afraid she was going to slap the captive.

"Let me try!" Sarah burst out.

The men looked at each other, then Mr. Carson said, "Go ahead, young 'un, if you think you can get anything out of her."

Sarah handed Elizabeth to Mrs. Carson and went to kneel in front of the silent woman. "Dulcie?" she questioned gently. "Are you Dulcie?"

★ Chapter Fifteen ★

The woman did not raise her eyes, but she stopped rocking and sat very still.

"If you are Dulcie," Sarah continued, "your husband has searched for you and Samuel ever since the day you were taken away from him."

The woman raised sad, empty eyes to Sarah's, eyes that were as scarred with suffering as her body.

"Marcus is waiting for you in Williamsburg," Sarah assured her. She saw a flicker of recognition at the name of Marcus. Then the eyes went blank again. "Would you like to go back to Marcus, Dulcie?" she added softly.

"Untie her!"

Sarah looked up to see Malinda standing in the doorway, both fists planted on her hips.

The captive looked around. Her eyes recognized Malinda. Then her face crumpled and she began to cry silently.

"This poor sick lady not be hurting anybody," Malinda said, crossing the room and kneeling in front of the captive. "If you will untie her, gentlemen, Malinda be taking care of her."

"Untie her," James Harrod said, coming down from upstairs.

When Gabe Carson had loosed the knots of the thong, Malinda put her arms around the captive, and the woman leaned against her, her shoulders shaking with silent sobs.

"She knows you!" Mr. Larkin exclaimed.

Malinda nodded. "She be the slave, Dulcie, who escaped from the Indians a few months back and came to Boonesborough," she explained. "She be free now, seeing as how her owners be killed by the Indians." Malinda looked around fiercely, silently daring anybody to challenge Dulcie's freedom.

Sarah felt tears sting her eyes. This was Dulcie! The years of pain and searching, of trusting and never giving up were now going to pay off. Oh, if only Marcus could know! Sarah didn't want to have to wait for Uncle Ethan to come back, and for the long journey to Williamsburg to be made, before Marcus knew that his beloved Dulcie had been found.

Dulcie lay against Malinda's big shoulder, her body still racked with the force of her silent grief.

"There now, it will be all right," Malinda soothed, patting her on the back. "Didn't Malinda hear the message of your drum and bring you food out there in the forest?"

Gabe Carson looked at Malinda sharply. "That was you opening the gates at night!"

"Malinda be taking this poor hungry woman something to eat, yes, sir!" she answered defiantly.

"You lied to me!" Mr. Carson accused angrily.

"No, sir," Malinda denied the accusation.

"Woman," he shouted, "I asked if you'd been out in the corral, and you said no!"

Malinda shook her head. "No, sir, Malinda said she be going after a fresh bucket of cold water, and she did," she corrected. "And she said she had nothing to do with horses, but she never said she did not go through the corral to the woods with a bucket of food!"

"Don't you sass him, you uppity slave!" Mrs. Carson spat out. "You know the gates are not to be opened! You ought to be horse whipped!"

"It's no more than you'd have done, Emma Carson, if you had discovered the woman, sick and hungry, hiding in the woods!" James Harrod interrupted.

Gabe Carson laughed, his anger easing. "You act fierce, Emma, but we all know that beneath that wolf's clothing, you're as gentle-hearted as a lamb!"

The men laughed with him, but Mrs. Carson did not seem amused.

"The question is, what do we do with our captive now?" Mark Larkin asked.

"I know her husband, Mr. Larkin," Sarah volunteered.

"But I thought everybody in the party she was traveling with was killed," he said, with a puzzled frown. "No, I believe there was one man who escaped to tell the story. Is that her husband? And how do you know him, Sarah?"

"No, sir," she corrected. "That's not her husband. Before Dulcie was sold, she had a husband back in Williamsburg, a freed slave named Marcus who serves as the gardener at the Governor's Palace. My Uncle Ethan knows him well. He's searched for Dulcie ever since she and their son were taken from him. I know he'd want her back, sir, whatever her condition."

"Your uncle is due back here any day," Colonel Harrod mused. "Perhaps he would take her back to Williamsburg with him. It seems the fair thing to do."

"Did you hear that, Dulcie?" Malinda crooned. "The colonel wants to send you home to your husband."

Dulcie looked up with pleading eyes. She shook her head violently, wringing her hands together in distress.

"She won't leave without her son," Malinda interpreted.

Sarah gently squeezed the woman's hand. "We may have seen Samuel, Dulcie," she told her. "He was with the Indians, carrying water for the braves."

"We'll find him, your Samuel," Malinda promised, as Dulcie began again to rock and to wail that tuneless song.

Sarah saw the woman's pain mirrored in the colonel's eyes. "Dulcie," he said sadly, "I wish I could help you, but if that was your son with Blackfish's braves, I'm afraid he's been carried back beyond the Ohio River to the Indian villages. Our scouts have reported that they're gone."

Malinda threw him a dark, unreadable look. "Come along, Dulcie," she said, helping the woman to her feet, "The colonel will do everything he can to find Samuel, won't you, Colonel? Now, let's be going to Mrs. Anabelle Reynolds's place where you can get a bath and some food."

Gabe Carson reached out to stop them, but Colonel Harrod shook his head. "Let them go, Gabe," he said. "The woman needs care, not punishment."

"We'll get you all cleaned up and see if we can find you something decent to wear," Malinda promised as they left the blockhouse. "Ain't neither one of Malinda's dresses gonna be fitting your skinny frame," she added, "but Mrs. Anabelle . . ."

Sarah took Elizabeth from Mrs. Carson and ran out of the building after Malinda and Dulcie. "She can have one of my dresses, Malinda," she offered when she caught up with them. "I have five."

"My, what a rich lady you be, missy!" Malinda said with a laugh. "But we do thank you kindly for your generous offer."

Sarah felt her face flush and was glad of the growing darkness. She hadn't meant to boast!

"Dulcie be such a little thing, missy, your dress just might be fitting her," Malinda said then. "Bring it down to the house, and we be trying it on."

Wondering which of her dresses she should give her, Sarah tried to measure Dulcie with her eyes as the two women walked on down to the blockhouse and disappeared inside. She looked at her cousin Abigail's brown hand-me-down that she was wearing. Ma insisted it still had a lot of wear in it and should not be wasted.

Obviously, the brown homespun dress wouldn't do, for it was already nearly too short for Sarah, and, besides, it was soiled from wear. On the other hand, if she went back to Williamsburg, she would need the serviceable gray dress Aunt Charity had made her for everyday and the fancy blue one she wore to church on Sundays.

That left only the soft red dress Ma had made her that first Christmas in Kentucky, when all they had to make cloth with was the lint from nettles mixed with buffalo wool. Would Ma object to her giving away the linsey-woolsey dress? Maybe she had better give Dulcie the serviceable gray one Aunt Charity had made. It was still like new, and she wanted Dulcie to have a nice dress to wear back to Williamsburg and Marcus.

How excited Marcus would be to see Dulcie again! But how sad to think that this worn, white-haired woman who could not, or would not, speak was the beautiful Dulcie who could sing like a nightingale! In her condition, would it be less cruel just to never tell him she had been found? What would Marcus do when he saw her?

If Sarah knew Marcus, he would put his arms around her and lead her home to his little house in Raccoon Trace where the black people of Williamsburg—free or slave— had their homes. There he would feed her and care for her and make her as comfortable as possible.

How would Dulcie feel to be reunited with her husband after all these years? Would she weep with joy, as she had when she saw Malinda tonight? Or would all the terrible things she had endured cause her to remain fearful and miserable the rest of her days?

Sarah carried Elizabeth inside the cabin, laid her on the bed, and handed her a wooden spoon. The baby cooed contentedly, waving the spoon in one little fist and following it with her blue eyes.

Smiling, Sarah went to the peg that held all her clothing and removed the gray dress. With it over her arm, she started to leave the cabin.

Ma looked up from her mending. "Where are you going with that dress, Sarah?" she asked.

Quickly, Sarah explained all that had happened and why she needed the dress. Surely Ma would understand! She had always been so generous.

Ma continued her sewing without comment, and Sarah was afraid she did not approve of what she planned to do.

★ Chapter Fifteen ★

"Take her one of those fresh white aprons I just finished, too, Sarah," she finally suggested.

"Yes, Ma," Sarah answered happily, glad to find that Ma had not changed in these last hard months.

Dulcie was sitting in Mrs. Reynolds's rocking chair wrapped in a quilt, by the time Sarah had finished her story for Ma and was able to get down to the blockhouse. Malinda was toweling the woman's hair dry.

Sarah held the dress out to her, but she made no move to accept it.

"Here, honey, now you put on this pretty dress," Malinda ordered. "Nothing makes a woman feel better than to get a new dress!" she chuckled.

Sarah recalled how eager she had been for Aunt Charity to finish the blue and the gray dresses when she first went to Williamsburg, and how glad she had been to wear something besides an ill-fitting hand-me-down.

Then she sighed, wishing there were something she could do to send Dulcie back to Marcus as she had been when she was taken from him.

Dulcie was here, though, and soon would be on her way back to her husband. That meant Sarah's promise to Marcus was half-fulfilled. Now she just had to find Samuel.

When Sarah went down to the blockhouse the next day for the girls' lessons, she found the Reynoldses out and Malinda sitting on the cold hearth, stringing green beans and chanting a song in some strange tongue.

Dulcie sat in a straight-backed chair in the corner. She was wearing Sarah's gray dress, which fit her fairly well.

Malinda stopped singing. "Well, missy . . ." she began.

"What was that song, Malinda?" Sarah interrupted.

"Oh, it just be an old island tune," Malinda answered vaguely.

"It is a haunting melody. What are the words?"

"They be straight out of the Bible, Miss Sarah, one of the psalms. Malinda just put the tune to them. And changed some of the words a little," she admitted. She began to sing again, this time in English. "As the deer panteth for the water brooks, so my soul longeth after Thee. My soul thirsteth for God, for the living God."

153

"I've never heard that before," Sarah said. "Is that all of it?"

Malinda busied herself with the beans, obviously embarrassed now. "No, there be more."

Sarah waited for her to sing the rest, but when she didn't, she said, "You know, Marcus told me that Dulcie could sing like a nightingale. I wonder if she ever sings now, anything besides that eerie wailing she was doing last night."

"She be doing it this afternoon, too. That be why Malinda started singing to her."

"Why does she do it, Malinda?"

"She be mourning for her son. It's a mixture of old island ways and the ways of the Indians, Malinda be thinking."

Sarah turned to the thin woman in the corner. "If you could tell us where the Indians held you captive, Dulcie, maybe we could find Sam," she said.

Dulcie looked up at her, then looked away.

"All she be knowing is that she swam two rivers to get to Boonesborough," Malinda answered for her.

"How did she manage to escape, Malinda?" Sarah asked. "And why didn't she take Samuel with her?"

Dulcie began to hum, that awful off-key hum that was almost a wail.

Malinda put her hands on the woman's shoulders. "It be all right, Dulcie," she murmured. "We be finding your Samuel soon now." And to the same tune as before, she sang, "Why art thou cast down, O my soul? And why art thou disquieted within me? Hope thou in God! For I shall yet praise Him who is . . . my God!"

When Dulcie quieted and sat staring at the wall, Malinda turned to Sarah. "She was sent to the creek with three Indian women to pound the flesh from deer hides. The Indians decided to take a swim when they be finished, and they be insisting that she swim with them. When Dulcie refused to remove her dress, the Indians threw her in, clothes and all. Then, as they be playing, laughing, and splashing each other, Dulcie went under the water and swam around a bend to the edge of the woods."

"And they never knew she was gone?" Sarah exclaimed.

Malinda shook her head. "Leastways, not while she could see them. She ran for miles through the woods until she came to a river. She swam across, and . . ." Malinda chuckled. "It be a good thing Dulcie be island born and be growing up swimming all the time!" she said.

"Isn't Boonesborough built right beside the river?" Sarah asked. "I think I heard Mrs. Reynolds say something about flooding there."

Malinda nodded. "Dulcie followed the big river—it must be the one they call Ohio—to where the Kentucky River empties into it. Then she followed the Kentucky to Boonesborough."

"And she left Boonesborough to try to find Sam," Sarah finished. "How did she think she could find him, Malinda, if she doesn't remember where they were? And how did she think she could rescue him from so many Indians by herself?"

"She be playing that drum, missy, hoping he hear and come to her, escape some way, like she did."

Dulcie murmured something, and Malinda bent closer to hear.

"What did she say?" Sarah asked.

"She say Sammy maybe want to stay with the Indians," Malinda explained. "Sometimes, they say captives be like that, especially the young ones. After living with the Indians, they begin to think like an Indian."

"But Samuel has only been with them a few months!" Sarah said. "And he must be nearly grown by now, too old to grow up thinking like an Indian. Why on earth would he want to stay a captive?"

"There be worse things for a boy, Miss Sarah, than spending his days fishing, hunting, riding horses, learning to shoot a bow and arrow. The Indian life be all the stuff young boys dream of doing all day long, especially if he be a slave boy!"

Sarah was stunned. All this time, she had thought of rescuing Samuel from a terrible situation, and now Malinda was saying he was happy where he was! It would break Marcus's heart, she thought, reaching into her pocket and pulling out the blue handkerchief that always brought him so close. It would just break his dear old heart to know that, after all these years of searching and longing, his son did not want to come home!

"Well, maybe Sammy just doesn't know what he wants," she began. "Maybe he's confused after . . ." She looked up to find Dulcie's eyes focused on her hands. Then she realized it was the handkerchief that held her attention. She knelt in front of Dulcie.

"This was Marcus's handkerchief," Sarah said, holding it out to her. "He would like to know you had it, Dulcie. He loves you very much." She swallowed hard, not wanting to give up her treasured gift, but knowing that what she had said to Dulcie was true.

Dulcie stared at the handkerchief with a strange look on her face, but she made no move to take it.

Malinda took the handkerchief, placed it in Dulcie's

hand, and closed her fingers around it. "This be your husband's, Dulcie," she said softly.

Dulcie looked up at Malinda, then switched her gaze to Sarah. Her dark eyes held a troubled question.

Sarah placed her hand over Dulcie's and squeezed it gently. "You keep it, Dulcie," she said. "Keep it to remind you of Marcus until you get back home to him."

Suddenly, Dulcie bent over the handkerchief and began to rock back and forth. She was muttering something over and over that Sarah couldn't understand.

"What is she saying, Malinda?"

"She be saying, 'I can't see him!' " Malinda interpreted.

"But what does she mean?" Sarah asked.

"Malinda think she mean she can't remember what her husband looks like anymore."

Sarah looked at the distressed woman, wondering what

it would be like to try to remember someone you loved and not be able to recall his or her face. She only had to look at the blue handkerchief, and Marcus's image came clearly into her mind—the kind dark eyes, the white curly hair, the mouth with creases made by the grin it so often wore. How awful not to be able to picture him! But Sarah had seen him only a few months ago, and it had been many years since Dulcie had laid eyes on her husband. What terrible memories lay between the day she had last seen Marcus and this moment? What awful experiences had crowded his face from her mind?

"There, now," Malinda comforted Dulcie. "Don't take on so! You'll be back with him soon, and you can refresh your memory of his face."

Dulcie looked up and studied Malinda. The pain Sarah saw in the woman's dark eyes cut through her. How terribly she must have suffered—was still suffering! As Mrs. Reynolds had said, who knew what the poor woman had endured, not only in her months with the Indians, but in the past years of slavery.

"Oh, there you are, Sarah!" Mrs. Reynolds exclaimed, coming into the cabin with her children. "We've been to visit Mrs. Carson's puppies. I'm sorry we're late."

"It's all right, Mrs. Reynolds," Sarah assured her, trying to turn her thoughts to the lessons she had prepared for the day. In the background, she could hear Malinda chanting her song from the Bible to Dulcie.

As soon as lessons were over, Sarah's thoughts returned to Dulcie. If only there were something more she could do to help her! If only she could take her to Marcus right now! But that was impossible. She left the blockhouse with Malinda's song ringing in her mind. She found herself humming it as she helped Ma prepare supper, and singing it to Jamie as she prepared him for bed.

"As the deer panteth for the water brooks, so my soul longeth after Thee!" she sang softly.

"What's the little deer doing, Sadie?" Jamie asked.

"Well, it means the deer is thirsty, Jamie. He wants a drink of water from the spring."

Jamie shook his head. "Deer asleep in the forest with his mother, Sadie," Jamie reminded her of their little story.

"That's right, sweets," she agreed, laying him on the trundle bed and bending over to give him a kiss on his forehead. "The baby deer is asleep beside his ma, all curled up in a thicket of cedar trees."

"Deer firsty, Sadie?" he persisted. Then, "Jamie firsty," he declared.

Sarah laughed and went to get him a drink of water. "Now, the little deer is not thirsty. He has been to the spring for a drink and he is going to sleep," she said firmly.

Jamie grinned, turned over on his stomach, and stuck his arms up under his pillow. Soon she could hear him breathing deeply.

Sarah wasn't sleepy. She wandered outside and over to the sweet gum tree by the animal pens, Malinda's song still running through her mind.

Malinda sang the little song like it came from the very depths of her being, Sarah thought as she sat on the wooden bench. "My soul thirsts for God, for the living God!" Malinda had sung. What did it mean to "thirst" for God, to long for Him as the deer pants for water?

Sarah knew how it felt for her mouth to be parched and her throat dry, to long for a refreshing drink of cold water from the spring. If she thirsted for God that way, would finding Him satisfy her longings as a drink of cold water quenched her thirst? Was that what the song meant?

Marcus and Pa found great satisfaction in God. They talked with Him like old friends, but she had always thought God was just out there somewhere, watching over the world in a remote sort of way.

And sometimes, she didn't think He did a very good job of it. At least, if she were God, she would do things a lot differently. She never would have let Dulcie and Sam be sold and taken away from Marcus, for instance. And she wouldn't have let the Indians take them captive. She wouldn't have let the Indians burn their buildings on Stoney Creek. She wouldn't have let Pa sell their farm in Miller's Forks, Virginia, in the first place!

Sarah wasn't God, though, and she really didn't think she understood Him very well.

She got up from the bench and walked over to pet the goats in the pen beside her. The youngest one rubbed his head against her hand, looking up at her with big, trusting eyes. She scratched the rough hair on the top of its head. "If I were God, I'd never let anything hurt you, little one," she murmured. "I wouldn't let anything hurt anything else anywhere in the world!" she vowed.

If, as Marcus said, God cared about folks the way He cared about every little old bird that fell to the ground, why did He allow hurt to come into the world? Or at least why didn't He help them find Samuel? Why didn't He restore Dulcie's mind so she could go back to Marcus well and happy? Why didn't He give Sarah some place where she could be at home, as she had been for the first eleven years of her life back in Miller's Forks?

"As the deer panteth for the water brooks, so my soul . . ."

she began softly. But God seemed as remote as those stars shining up there in the sky. How had Pa and Marcus come to know Him so well? Why did they feel so close to Him?

Suddenly, Sarah remembered a night she had run to Marcus for help with her overwhelming sorrow. "When the Son of God leaves the throne of glory and lays Himself down on this old dirt just like a bridge for you to walk on back to God," he had said, "you have to open yourself up to a special relationship with Him."

Was that what she wanted? Was that why there was a big empty space inside her? Maybe it was a God-shaped space that nothing else could fill. But what could she do about it? How could she open herself up to Him, as Marcus said?

Sarah looked up at the stars, twinkling coldly so far above. She sighed. They weren't any closer than they had been a few moments ago. And, no matter what Marcus or Pa said, neither was God.

After a week of healing and no further Indian attacks, Pa was up and pacing restlessly around the cabin. "I may not be able to swing an axe yet, but I can use a hammer and I can make shingles with an adz," he declared one morning, and he left the cabin. Sarah watched him enter the Larkins' cabin on down the row.

She wondered if she should ask him now to help her search for Sam. She had waited, thinking he wasn't able to travel, but maybe he would welcome the opportunity to do something outside the stockade now that he was better and it seemed the threat from the Indians was gone.

When Pa came back to the cabin, though, he had plans of his own to share. "The Larkins, Luke, and I are heading out in the morning for Stoney Creek to start rebuilding our cabins," he announced. "It'll be winter before we know it, and the Indians are gone for now. I aim for us to be back on our own land before snow flies!"

★ Reunion in Kentucky ★

The next morning, Sarah watched, with tears in her eyes, as Pa and Luke rode off with Mr. Larkin and his boys. Not only was she concerned for their safety, but now she also had no one to help her find Sam.

For two days, Sarah's frustration grew. She knew she couldn't travel through the wilderness alone. How on earth was she going to find Sam? Finally, she decided she would just have to ask James Harrod to help her. She was on her way to his blockhouse when the gates of the fort opened and her Uncle Ethan and the Little Captain rode inside.

Uncle Ethan looked weary, and his usually neat black coat and knee breeches were much the worse for wear. Sarah was sure his white stockings would have to be thrown away. There would be no way to mend or whiten the ragged, travel-stained things!

Sarah recognized the Little Captain at once. Wearing buckskin breeches and the blue soldier's coat with just one remaining brass button, he looked exactly as he had the first time she had seen him, standing beside their campfire holding a knife in one hand and a piece of Ma's corn bread in the other. Now, the mane of a brown and white horse was wrapped around one hand, and he held a rifle in the other. His black eyes recognized her, and she nodded in greeting.

"Any Indian sign here about?" Colonel Harrod asked as her uncle and his companion dismounted.

"Nothing recent," Uncle Ethan answered. He removed a small pack from Jake's back and handed the horse's reins to the youngest Carson boy. Then, seeing her standing there, he said, "Hello, Sarah. How are Della and the baby? And where's your pa?"

"Ma and Elizabeth are much better, thank you, Uncle

Ethan," she answered, "and Pa and Luke left two days ago with the Larkin men to go back to Stoney Creek and start rebuilding. He surely was glad to have those hinges and nails we brought from Williamsburg, Uncle Ethan!" she added. "Remember how heavy my traveling bag was?"

He made a face. "I reckon I do!" he said. "I thought you had a ton of bricks in that bag!"

Sarah laughed. Then she remembered where she had been headed when her uncle rode into the fort.

"I need to talk with you, Uncle Ethan," she said.

"Of course," he agreed. "What is it?"

"Uncle Ethan, we have found Marcus's wife! She's down in the George Rogers Clark blockhouse with the Reynolds family, and we're pretty sure Sam was here during the siege, carrying water for the braves. Now they've taken him back with them," she finished breathlessly.

"And you're proposing that I go after him? Is that it, Sarah?" her uncle asked, a grin playing at the corners of his mouth.

"Oh, Uncle Ethan, would you?" Sarah pleaded. "Then you could take him and Dulcie with you back to Marcus. Think how happy he would be to get them back after all these years! I just wish I could see his face. . . . "

"Sarah," her uncle broke in, "do you have any idea what you are asking? I just came from Fort Boonesborough. There were hundreds of Indians in Blackfish's war party, enough to paralyze both Fort Boonesborough and Fort Harrod for nearly two weeks!"

"But, Uncle Ethan, we held them off!" she answered. "I helped load guns, and . . . "

He smiled. "I don't doubt it, Sarah," he said.

Colonel Harrod chuckled. "Young lady, without the

165

protection of these log walls, we'd all be dead and scalped by now!" he said. "There aren't enough men in all of Kentucky to fight Blackfish and his braves in open country."

"But there must be something we can do!" she said desperately.

"Sarah," her uncle said, "we don't even know where Sam would be. The Indians have lots of war parties. He could be with any of them."

"The Little Captain know." Sarah jumped at the sound of the Indian scout's voice beside her. He grinned down at her. "Little Captain no hurt young miss. Your ma make good corn bread!" he assured her, rubbing his stomach. "Little Captain hungry now! Colonel Strong Arms hungry, too," he added persuasively.

"Strong Arms?" Sarah repeated. Did the Indian think her uncle's name was Armstrong because he had strong arms? She had heard that the Indians named their children after the first thing they noticed about the baby or after the first important deed they did.

Uncle Ethan laughed. "Is Della able to cook, Sarah?" he asked, and at her nod, said, "See if she will fix us something. Hardtack and jerky keep us alive on the trail, but they surely aren't very tasty! I've found myself dreaming of sour old Hester's sweet cooking!"

Instantly, a vision of the Armstrong's dining table back in Williamsburg came into Sarah's mind—crisp fried chicken and milk gravy, mashed potatoes dripping fresh-churned butter, blackberry cobbler. She pushed the tantalizing thoughts away. "But, Uncle Ethan, what about Sam?"

"Do as I ask, Sarah, and we will discuss it over some

nourishing food," he said firmly, turning to follow Colonel Harrod to his blockhouse. "I should be freshened up by the time it's ready."

Disappointed, Sarah went back to the cabin to help Ma fix a meal for her uncle and the Little Captain. Then she sat watching as the men ate, hungrily and silently.

When they had finished, the Little Captain arose and gave a loud belch. Sarah saw Ma flinch. "Good!" he said. "Little Captain much hungry. Food much good!" His eyes fell on the silver disk he had given Ma the last time she had fed him, still dangling from its rawhide string around her neck. A wide smile cut across the Indian's swarthy face. "You like?" he asked, pointing to the necklace.

Ma reached up to touch the disk. "It saved my life once," she said softly. "Thank you, Little Captain."

He studied her for a moment, then nodded, and left the cabin. From where she sat, Sarah could see him walking toward the Clark blockhouse.

If he wanted to see Colonel Clark, he would be disappointed, for the red-haired colonel had not returned from taking his Indian prisoners to Fort Pitt. Sarah hoped the Little Captain would not frighten the Reynolds family or Dulcie. After her ordeal with the Indians, Dulcie might be scared of all of them. Then she grinned, thinking of what Malinda might do or say to him.

"Now, Sarah, tell me all you know about Marcus's family," Uncle Ethan said, pushing his empty plate aside and folding his arms on the table.

Quickly, Sarah told him all she knew about their capture by the Indians, Dulcie's ultimate escape, Malinda and the drum, and their brief glimpse of the young black man with the Indians who had besieged the fort.

"Could I have another cup of that coffee, Della?" he asked. "You always did make the best coffee in Virginia!"

Sarah saw Ma blush. "Why, thank you, Ethan!" she said, filling his cup. "It's the egg shells I boil with it," she confided, offering him the sugar bowl.

He shook his head. "With sugar so rare on the trail, I've learned to drink it black," he explained.

"Uncle Ethan, will you try to get Sam back?" Sarah broke in impatiently. "Marcus . . . "

"I am well aware of how much his son means to Marcus," her uncle said. "And I would do anything possible to get the boy back for him. But, given the manpower available and the risk involved, I doubt there's much I can do. I just don't want you to get your hopes too high."

Sarah stared at her hands on the table top. She was sure if it had been Luke who was a captive or one of Uncle Ethan's own daughters, Uncle Ethan would be on his way to get them right now.

He reached over and patted her hand. "I will do my best, Sarah," he promised. "But I won't endanger the protection of the fort by taking too many men away from its defense, and I won't take anybody but volunteers." He sighed deeply. "We will need some way to get him out away from the Indians, and they won't be allowing him too much freedom, is my guess, though you never know what they will do. They let Daniel Boone roam at will, I'm told. That was how he was able to make his escape to warn the forts of their planned attack earlier this year."

Uncle Ethan returned to Colonel Harrod's blockhouse, and Sarah sat pondering his words, her hopes low. Then she remembered the drum. Did Sam know the language of the drum, as Dulcie and Malinda did? He had been born in

Virginia, not in Barbados, but maybe Dulcie had taught him to understand the language of the drums.

"Why do you think his ma be spending night after night out there in the woods? She trying to contact him by playing her drum," Malinda responded sarcastically when Sarah asked the question a few minutes later down in the Reynolds' cabin. "Malinda think you be cooking up something, young miss," she said then, studying her out of serious dark eyes.

"It's just that Uncle Ethan said that if they went after Sam, they would need some way to get him away from the Indians, and I thought of the drum. If Dulcie . . . " She stopped, looking at the slender, white-haired woman sitting in Mrs. Reynolds's rocking chair, staring into the unlit fireplace. "Or if you, Malinda, could go with the men and signal to Sam from the woods, maybe he would figure out some way to escape and meet Uncle Ethan. My uncle knows Sam's father, you know."

Malinda did not reply, and Sarah added quickly, "I'd go with you."

"Oh, that be comforting, missy!" Malinda said with a half smile. "It be very comforting to know that when 300 Indians capture Malinda, you be there to protect her!"

"Oh, Malinda," Sarah burst out in exasperation, "Uncle Ethan and the others will be there to protect us!"

Malinda studied her again. "Let me talk to Dulcie about it alone," she suggested finally. "I be letting you know what she say."

Sarah knew she had been dismissed. She had no choice but to go back to the Moore cabin and wait for Malinda's answer.

Before Malinda came, Uncle Ethan returned to the

cabin where Sarah and Ma were getting Elizabeth and Jamie ready for bed. "I can only get five volunteers to go with me after Sam," he reported, "plus the Little Captain, who claims to know where they will have taken him. We'll leave at dawn. But, Sarah, don't get your hopes up too high," he cautioned.

Sarah stared at him in dismay. "But, Uncle Ethan, how will only six men and one Indian guide get Sam away from so many Indians?" How heartbroken Marcus would be if he knew how close they had come, only to fail!

"Indians! Bang! Bang!" Jamie cried, jumping out of the trundle bed to race around the room.

"Jamie!" Ma scolded. She laid Elizabeth on the big bed and reached for the little boy.

"Right now, I can't think of a plan that would have the chance of a snowball in July!" Uncle Ethan admitted, his warm brown eyes troubled as he snatched up Jamie and sat down with him in his lap. "We certainly can't overwhelm them! We'll just have to outsmart them somehow!"

"We be going after Dulcie's Samuel," Malinda said to Sarah from the doorway. "Good evening, sir, ma'am," she added politely.

Uncle Ethan looked at Malinda, then at Sarah. "What's going on?"

Sarah explained about the drum. "If we could get within Sam's hearing, he just might come in answer to his mother's drum message," she finished.

For several seconds, her uncle roughhoused with a giggling Jamie, and Sarah began to fear that he wouldn't even consider her plan. Then he looked up at her and smiled. "It just might work!" he agreed, laying Jamie on the trundle bed and giving him one last tickle on the ribs.

"Anyway, it's the best idea I've heard so far. We'll have to work fast. If Sam can hear the drum, the Indians will, too, and they will be quick to investigate."

He turned to Malinda. "We leave at dawn. Meet us at the front gates, dressed and packed for a hard, fast journey," he said.

Malinda nodded and left the cabin.

"I want to go with you, Uncle Ethan," Sarah said. She heard Ma gasp from over by the fireplace where she was putting away the supper dishes.

"Sarah, that's out of the question!" she said, her back stiff and unyielding as she arranged the dishes on the mantel.

Her uncle smiled. "I wouldn't want to risk losing you, Sarah," he said, "now that I know what a brilliant military strategist you are!"

Sarah answered with a pout, and he reached over to tug one of her long, brown braids. "Your Aunt Charity would skin me alive, young lady, if I so much as thought about taking you with me," he assured her, "not to mention what Meggie would do!"

Sarah still didn't answer him. From the corner of her eye, she saw him smile at Ma. "You've come up with the only plan that seems to have half a chance of working, Sarah," he said. "Be content with that."

As he left the cabin, Sarah's mind churned with ways that she might get him and Ma to change their minds before dawn.

Sarah awoke to the pounding of a heavy late September rain on the roof. It was still dark beyond the cabin window.

Nothing feels so good as to turn over in a warm, dry bed and go back to sleep while the rain falls outside, she thought, doing just that.

When she awoke again, the rain was still coming down, and it wasn't much lighter outside. But Ma had built a fire in the fireplace and was starting breakfast.

Even though the sun didn't seem to have any intention of showing its face, it had to be past the time for sun-rise. Sarah jumped out of bed and pulled on her brown dress. "Why didn't you call me, Ma?" she asked. "Uncle Ethan was leaving at dawn!"

"Calm down, dear. Your uncle sent word they're not going till the rain lets up," Ma said, concentrating on whatever she was stirring in the iron skillet. "Besides, you weren't going anywhere. Remember?"

Sarah sighed. Obviously, Ma had not changed her mind. But if Uncle Ethan weren't leaving until the rain let up, maybe there was still time to persuade her, Sarah thought as she fixed Jamie a plate of deer sausage, biscuits, and gravy. Then she fed Elizabeth.

After she and Ma had eaten and washed the dishes, she stood in the doorway looking out through the curtain of water pouring off the roof. She could hear it overflowing the rain barrel at the corner of the cabin. The rain sounded like it might never let up! How long would it be before her uncle kept his promise to go after Sam?

Sarah reached for a shawl on a wooden peg by the door and threw it over her head and shoulders. "I'm going down to the Reynolds', Ma!" she called, stepping out into the downpour before her mother could protest. As she dodged puddles, she could feel the rain reaching through the shawl. Before she got halfway to the blockhouse only two doors away, she was soaked through.

Mrs. Reynolds and the three girls looked up from the table. They were taking turns using the scissors to cut quilt squares from some bright-colored cloth by the light of a fat tallow candle.

Sarah threw a quick glance around the room, but no one else was there, except the baby cooing in his cradle. "Where's Malinda?" she asked. "And Dulcie?"

"Why, they left with your uncle and the others at dawn, what there was of it," Mrs. Reynolds answered. "You know. To go find Dulcie's boy."

Sarah shook her head.

"Yes, they did, Sarah," Mrs. Reynolds insisted. "Both of them. They packed some provisions and that drum of Dulcie's. Malinda found it out in the graveyard, and . . . "

★ Chapter Eighteen ★

"But, Mrs. Reynolds," Sarah broke in, "Uncle Ethan postponed the trip until the rain stops. He and the men are still here."

Mrs. Reynolds's blue eyes widened. "Are you sure, Sarah?" she asked.

"Yes, ma'am. My uncle sent word to Ma this morning that they wouldn't be going until the rain was over. He surely sent word to Malinda, too."

"Could he have changed his mind later?" Mrs. Reynolds suggested hopefully. "Maybe when he saw Malinda and Dulcie all ready to go . . . "

Sarah shook her head again. "I don't think so, Mrs. Reynolds. Uncle Ethan hates traveling in the rain. And once he sets his mind, it's awfully hard to get him to change it. I've been trying to get him to let me go with them after Sam, but he said no, and I don't have much hope of him changing his mind about that."

Mrs. Reynolds chewed her lip. "Then Malinda and Dulcie are out there somewhere alone," she said finally. "Sarah, what are we going to do? Even if they make it through the wilderness, they won't have a chance against the Indians! Oh, Sarah, Malinda is just like part of our family! And that poor Dulcie!"

"With Dulcie to look after," Sarah said, "Malinda's got her hands full without Indians."

"Malinda's smart, Ma," Felicity comforted. "She always knows what to do. She'll manage."

"But Indians, Felicity!" Caroline reminded her sister. "There are hundreds of them! Malinda can't fight all those Indians."

Little Lucy began to cry. "I want Malinda back here right now!" she sobbed.

"Hush, Lucy!" Felicity commanded. "Malinda will outsmart those Indians and be back here before we know it, with Sam and Dulcie. Just you wait and see."

Sarah hoped Felicity was right. All the same, though, she thought she'd better let her uncle know about this new turn of events.

"I'm going to see Uncle Ethan," she said. "Maybe he and the men will go after them when they hear what has happened."

"Thank you, Sarah," Mrs. Reynolds said. "Please let me know what your uncle decides."

"Yes, ma'am, I will," she promised, running back out into the rain.

When she reached Colonel Harrod's blockhouse, though, she found that, true to his history, Uncle Ethan wasn't ready to change his plans.

"Sarah, I asked these men to risk their lives going into Indian territory to rescue Marcus's son, but I didn't ask them to volunteer for the lung fever or to drown in a downpour like this!" he said firmly.

"But, Uncle Ethan, they're out there all alone in the wilderness!" she cried. "Two helpless women!"

Her uncle chuckled. "I don't for a moment think Malinda is helpless," he said. "That woman could out-maneuver the devil himself! And Dulcie has lived in the wilderness alone for weeks on end. If Malinda has let that poor, deluded woman convince her they must go immediately on an errand that could just as well wait a few hours, or even a few days, I can't help it. Sarah, I will not ask these men to risk any more."

"But Malinda and Dulcie . . . " she began.

" . . . are on a foolish mission that could have waited for

the rain to stop," he finished for her. "The boy has been with the Indians for months now. Two or three more days won't make much difference," he added. "Sarah, I promise you I will do everything in my power to overtake them as soon as the weather permits. And with us on horseback and the two women afoot, it shouldn't take us long to catch up with them. We'll be with them before they get to the Ohio River, long before they reach any Indian villages," he said, patting her hand reassuringly.

Sarah studied his concerned brown eyes and saw determination under their warmth. She had seen that look before, and she knew that further argument was useless. Her uncle's mind was set. There was nothing she could do.

"But I've got to do something!" she said aloud as she left the blockhouse and headed back toward her family's cabin. She couldn't let Marcus down now when they were so close to getting his family back.

"The Little Captain can lead you to them," a voice said beside her.

"You can find Malinda and Dulcie?" Sarah asked, wondering the reasons for his sudden generous offer. Was this a trick like the Indians had tried to pull on Pa and Colonel Harrod the day Pa was wounded? Was he attempting to lure her away from the fort so he could . . . what? Kill her? But he'd had plenty of opportunity to do that—at their camp two years ago, here inside the fort as she wandered around by herself, out in the cemetery where she went to think and dream any time she found the gates ajar.

"Little Captain no hurt," he said, as though he had read her thoughts. "Black women be afraid of Little Captain if he come upon them in woods," he explained. "No be afraid of young miss."

It made sense, she decided, moving under the protective overhang of the nearest cabin roof. And here was her chance to help Marcus when nobody else would. Oh, she knew Uncle Ethan would keep his promise, when the rain let up. But this rain showed no sign of letting up soon. It could be days before her uncle led his rescue party into the woods. By then, who knew what dreadful thing might have happened to Malinda and Dulcie?

"Ma would never agree to it!" she said aloud. "Not in a million years."

Marcus's sad face came to her mind, his dark eyes troubled. He had been so good to her when she was a stranger in Williamsburg. His wise counsel had helped her through many hard times. And he had risked much to try to help her find Gabrielle before she was deported back to France. Sarah loved Marcus like he was a member of her own family, and she would do anything possible to help him get back the wife and son he had searched for all these years.

Then there was Malinda and the huge debt she owed her for saving Ma and Elizabeth. Surely Ma would understand why she had to go! And she and the Little Captain would certainly be back almost before anyone realized they were gone, bringing Malinda, Dulcie, and Sam with them.

Sarah would have to go back to the cabin, though, to get provisions, and she would need some protection from the rain.

She glanced at the Little Captain, standing there oblivious to the rain pouring over him, and she realized that he had a deerskin cape around his shoulders. The hair of the deer was turned to the inside for warmth, and the smooth, tanned leather side was turned out to keep off the rain.

Could she use one of the deerskins Pa had wrapped around their bed covers and spare clothing to keep them dry on the trip into Kentucky? She supposed he had taken at least one of them to make a shelter on Stoney Creek until he could get a new cabin built.

She would look for a deerskin, she decided. The cabin was so small, if one were there, it shouldn't be hard to find. Then all she would need to worry about was how to get Gracie and get away from the fort without being seen.

"All right," she finally said to the Little Captain, "I'll go."

The Indian studied her for several seconds. "Which horse young miss ride?" he asked finally. "Little Captain get horses. Wait at forest."

"My Gracie is the little brown mare with the white forelegs and small white star on her forehead," she answered.

The Indian's fierce eyes burned into hers. "Young miss no come, Little Captain no go!" he warned sternly.

Sarah nodded again. "I'll be there," she promised, watching him head toward the corral gates. About halfway there, he disappeared like mist into the rain.

Suddenly, Sarah remembered that Ma was in the cabin. How was she going to get into the cabin, get what she needed, and get out again without Ma finding out what she was about to do?

Then, in amazement, Sarah saw Ma leaving the cabin. She had a quilt thrown over her, the baby, and Jamie, carrying each of them on a hip. She was headed toward the Larkins' cabin. Sarah guessed that Jamie had begged all morning to go see "Roofie." She supposed Ma had had all she could take of being shut up in that cabin, a prisoner of the rain. Finally, she must have decided to humor Jamie and go visiting the Larkins, rain or no rain. Was this a sign from heaven that she was doing the right thing in going after Malinda and Dulcie?

Sarah dashed to the cabin, wrapped some corn bread and cold baked potatoes in a clean dish cloth, and put them into her small deerskin bag. Then she added a dress, underclothes, and a shawl. She found a deerskin under the bed where Pa had stored it, and threw it around her shoulders.

It would be useless to change her wet clothing, she decided as she hunted for something to write on, for she would be wet again in minutes in spite of the deerskin.

"It's also useless to hunt for a piece of paper around here," she said aloud. There just wasn't any. But she had to leave Ma a note explaining where she had gone! Then her glance fell on her precious copy of *The Pilgrim's Progress*. Desperately, she cast another look around the room. Then, wincing, she carefully tore out a blank page from the back of the book, and scribbled a note to Ma on it. She propped the paper on the mantel against Ma's china teapot where she would be sure to see it.

Sarah looked around the tiny cabin, wondering when she would see it again. Just thinking of going off into the wilderness on her own with an Indian she hardly knew made the cramped room suddenly seem very cozy.

Resolutely, Sarah pushed the thought aside, left the cabin, and headed for the corral gates.

Sarah cast fearful glances into the murky depths of the wet forest on either side of them. The trees rose up tall and dark, and so big around she could not circle them with both arms. A whole tribe of Indians could be hiding among them without being seen. Who knew what dangers lurked there!

She urged Gracie forward to close the gap between her and the Little Captain. He rode in silence ahead of her, guiding his saddleless, spotted horse down the old Indian trail by the touch of his hand and the pressure of his knees.

The rain had slowed to a cold drizzle that fell straight down from a gray, sunless sky. Breathing in the damp air, she could smell the musky leaf mold of many seasons and, above it, the faint scent of the beginnings of another autumn that would add its own layer of dying leaves to the thick mat beneath the trees.

Sarah shivered under her makeshift deerskin cape. Would she, too, die here in the dark forest, killed by some

Indian brave, or even at the hand of the Little Captain himself? She knew nothing about this Indian except that he liked Daniel Boone and Ma's cooking, and his silver disk had saved Ma's life. How foolish she had been to come trustingly into the wilderness with him! Could she actually lie down and go to sleep tonight, trusting this stranger to protect her, trusting him not to kill her while she slept?

The Little Captain appeared to be more civilized than most Indians, with his talk of "General S'washington" and his ability to speak many languages. But he was still an Indian, with an Indian's way of looking at things. And though he claimed to be loyal to the Patriot cause, he admitted little love for the settlers who were coming into Kentucky and making farms out of his hunting grounds. Why should he care about Malinda and Dulcie, or Sam? Why had he offered to lead her to them?

Sarah looked behind her to where the trail disappeared into the trees. Should she turn Gracie and head back the way they had come? Should she try to make it back to the fort on her own before something terrible happened to her? She peered into the forest, then looked at the Indian riding ahead of her. Which did she fear the most?

As though he knew she was thinking about him, the Little Captain turned and looked at her. "The Colonel Strong Arms will be here soon," he predicted. He studied the bleak, gray sky and seemed to find answers where Sarah saw nothing but the promise of more cold rain. "He catch up before the moon looks down on the Little Captain and young miss," he said.

Sarah nodded, hoping with all her being that he was right, that her uncle would be there before nightfall, that she would not have to spend the night out here in the forest with only the Little Captain for company.

Uncle Ethan was sure to be very angry with her, though. He had been understanding about her involvement with Gabrielle. He had forgiven her for going off on her own to say good-bye to Gabrielle before she was deported to France. He had even sent Marcus after her to protect her and to bring her home. But this time . . .

"The Colonel Strong Arms be much angry, Little Captain think," the Indian commented. "He say, 'Wait till rain stop.' We no wait," he added matter-of-factly, with a sassy grin that sat strangely on his fierce features.

Suddenly, she had to know. "Why did you offer to lead me out here against his wishes?" she asked.

"Little Captain owe Malinda for taking British bullet out of arm over at Boonesborough. Little Captain always pay his debts!" he answered proudly.

That was true, Sarah thought. He had paid Ma for supper that first night on Stoney Creek by giving her the silver disk.

"Little Captain know the Colonel Strong Arms come after young miss, rain or no rain," he continued, throwing her that same sassy grin. "The Colonel Strong Arms may kill, but he won't eat Little Captain and young miss! That what Big Turtle always say." Then his grin faded. "The Colonel Strong Arms be much angry," he repeated solemnly, nudging his horse to a trot and moving ahead of her again.

Sarah swallowed hard, knowing the Little Captain was right. She doubted that her uncle would be as willing to forgive this deliberate disobedience of both his and Ma's orders, especially since she was supposed to have learned the value of obedience back in Williamsburg.

An hour or so later, she heard the sound of horses' hooves and the rattle of gear behind them. She turned to see five or six men riding single file down the trail. Three of them each led a riderless horse. Then she saw her uncle at the head of the column, and she didn't know whether to shout for joy or throw herself at his feet to beg for mercy.

"Your ma is worried sick, Sarah Moore," he said through clenched teeth as he caught up with her. "Make no mistake about it, young lady, if Della doesn't punish you for this little escapade, I will!"

He passed her and rode up beside the Little Captain. She heard him speaking just as angrily to the Indian, who pulled himself up to his full height and rode off into the forest. And though they rode for another two or three hours, the Little Captain did not reappear until they had pitched camp for the night and the smells of squirrel frying and journey cake baking filled the air.

The rain had stopped at last, and Sarah stood by the fire trying to dry her clothes and warm herself against the evening's chill, when the Little Captain walked into the camp. As though nothing had happened, he filled a plate with food and sat down near the campfire to eat.

Sarah wasn't hungry. She had a big empty space inside her, but it had nothing to do with a longing for food. It was a hunger for forgiveness, a longing to be told that she had done right in going into the wilderness on her own. She had so wanted to help find Samuel! Marcus had been so good to her, and she wanted to do something special for him. She wanted to take Samuel and Dulcie back to him, to see the light of joy come into his eyes as he realized his loved ones were home at last.

★ Chapter Nineteen ★

Deep inside, though, she knew she should not have gone on her own with the Little Captain. She had disobeyed Ma and caused her great distress. And though her uncle encouraged her to eat and helped her prepare a bed, his brown eyes did not kindle with their usual warmth when he looked at her. In fact, he seemed to avoid looking at her. He was polite and proper and very cold.

Finally, she could stand it no longer. She went to kneel at her uncle's side as he ate, sitting on a log a little distance from the other men. "Uncle Ethan, I am sorry," she began. "I know I shouldn't have gone off this way, but I wanted to help find . . . "

"It won't work this time, Sarah," he interrupted coldly. "You are a very headstrong and rebellious young lady. You insist on doing things your own way, and when you are caught, you think an apology and a few tears will set things right."

"But, Uncle Ethan, I really am. . . . "

"It will not work, Sarah," he repeated firmly. "This time you will be punished, as soon as we get back to the fort. I would send you back now, but I can't spare anyone to take you. So you will have to stay with us until our mission is completed. Eat your supper and go to bed."

Sarah knelt there a moment, feeling as though he had slapped her. She couldn't believe that her usually kind and loving uncle wouldn't even let her say she was sorry!

"Where do you think we'll overtake 'em, Colonel?" one of the men asked. "Do you think the women will reach the Ohio River before we catch up with them?"

"It's more likely that we will find them on one side or the other of the Kentucky," Uncle Ethan answered, beginning a complicated explanation of the time required for travel afoot and on horseback.

Sarah arose, and, casting a glance around to be sure all the men were settled around the fire, she picked up her bag and went off behind a big cedar tree to change into dry clothing. When she had put on the red linsey-woolsey dress Ma had made her, she took her shawl from the bag and wrapped it around her.

She had been soaked to the skin, but she threw her wet underthings into the bag. She couldn't spread them out to dry where the men could see them, though she doubted they would notice. When she spread her dress out near the campfire to dry, they all acted as though she didn't exist.

Sarah wished she had someone to talk to, someone who would listen to her side of the story and understand that she had wanted to play a major role in rescuing Marcus's son and restoring him to his father. She wished Marcus were here right now. He always knew how to make her feel better about things. He would understand about wanting to help a friend.

Suddenly, Marcus's words came into her mind from a night back in Williamsburg when she had run to him for advice. She hadn't told the old man what she planned to do, only that she needed to help a friend. He had said, "Friends are mighty important in this mixed-up ole world," and he had gone on to tell her that God had created mankind simply because He wanted friends.

How had Marcus put it? "God wants each one of us to be His personal friend, to hold a conversation with Him all day long, every day of our lives, just like I'm talking with you, here," he had said. Then he had talked about God loving the world so much that He gave His only Son, Jesus Christ, to die on the cross so that whosoever believed in

Him would not perish. Those were the words from John 3:16 that always brought tears to Pa's eyes when he read them from his big black Bible.

"I just can't get over Him loving a no-account rascal like me that much!" Marcus had said. Sarah recalled his words as though he had spoken them to her yesterday. "If I was the only human being alive on this Earth, Jesus would have died for me! That makes Him and me pretty special friends, I reckon."

Did that mean she had a friend out there after all? Could she really talk with God just like she talked with Marcus? She prayed sometimes, like when Ma and Elizabeth were so sick, and when Pa had been wounded by the Indians, and when she thought of Nate out there somewhere fighting the British. But God still seemed as remote to her as those stars shining dimly up there in the night sky.

Then, all at once, she understood. God seemed remote to her because she had never made friends with Him as Marcus and Pa had done; she had never accepted His forgiveness. It was like Jamie and the nonpareils. God held out His gift of forgiveness to "whosoever" would accept it, no matter what they had done. But it wasn't hers until she reached out and took it!

Sarah took a deep breath. What did she have to lose? "God, I accept it right now," she whispered. Then the words began to pour out like tears. "God, I have done terrible things. Uncle Ethan is right. I am a headstrong and rebellious person. I reckon You know that. All my life, I've done things my way instead of the way I'm told to do them. I reckon You know that, too. And when I've been sorry for what I've done, it's mostly been because I didn't

want to face the consequences.

"This time, God, no matter what Uncle Ethan believes, I truly am sorry," she continued. "Most of all, I want Your forgiveness, for all the times I have disobeyed You. I want to talk with You, God, and listen to You all day long, every day of my life, as Marcus and Pa do," she whispered. "I want to trust You with all my heart and acknowledge You in all my ways. I want You to direct my paths," she quoted from the verses Marcus had shared with her just before she left Williamsburg.

Suddenly, she had run out of words. She didn't know what else to say. Then as she lay there with the tears flowing down onto her crossed arms, she felt a warm, sweet peace begin deep inside and spread through her, filling all her empty spaces. "Oh, thank You!" she breathed, knowing, beyond a shadow of a doubt, that she had been forgiven, that she belonged to her Creator in a way she never had before.

She lay there, her mind and her body floating in a cloud of peace. She still faced asking Ma and Uncle Ethan to forgive her. She still must endure the punishment one or both of them meted out to her. Uncle Ethan had promised she would be punished, and she knew he would make sure his word was kept. Yet, even her bones seemed to melt into a peace that none of those outside things could disturb.

Finally, she realized she had not ended her prayer. What else should she say? She wiped away the last of her tears. Then she remembered the way Pa always closed a prayer. "In the name of Jesus, our Savior, Amen," she finished.

Sarah stretched out on the cedar boughs. It was incredible how peaceful, how contented she felt out there on her makeshift bed in the middle of the wilderness! And, oblivious to the men's voices over by the campfire, oblivious to the dangers of the forest around her, Sarah sank into a deep, refreshing sleep.

It wasn't the drum that called her from sleep early the next morning. When she was fully awake, Sarah realized that the drum had been a part of her dreams for a long time during the night. It was the sudden silence that had roused her.

"That drum stopped right in the middle of something!" she heard Caleb say.

"Either something caught the drummer's attention or something happened to the drummer," Uncle Ethan agreed. "Where would you say those Indians are, Little Captain?"

"Indians across river," the Little Captain answered confidently. "Drum not Indian."

"Not Indian? How do you know?" Uncle Ethan asked.

"Drum speak with strange tongue. Little Captain no understand. Not Indian," he repeated firmly.

"It's Dulcie or Malinda," Sarah said. "The language of

the drum is from Barbados. They're trying to call Samuel."

Her uncle nodded. "Where are they, Little Captain?" he asked.

"Little Captain say near river you call Ken-tuck-ee."

"The Kentucky. Yes, that's about where they should be by now. Can you lead us to them?" Uncle Ethan asked.

The Indian grunted. "Little Captain lead. Colonel Strong Arms follow. Soon see," he answered smugly, moving toward the bushes where the horses were tied.

Soon they were mounted and riding single file down a narrow trail behind the Little Captain. Before long, Sarah could hear the sound of a river in the distance. Then suddenly, the Little Captain motioned for them to leave the trail and go into the forest. Horses and riders melted into the trees like shadows.

Sarah reined Gracie in behind a cedar tree and sat still, straining to hear above the pounding of her heart. What had the Little Captain heard that had alarmed him? Suddenly Sarah heard feet padding down the trail toward them. How many were there? Could their small party defend? . . .

Then she saw them. Malinda led the way, carrying a small bundle over her arm. Dulcie followed, her face lit up like a candle burned inside it, holding tightly to the hand of a nearly grown boy dressed in buckskin and moccasins.

"It's Malinda and Dulcie, and they've got Sam!" Sarah called to her uncle. She urged Gracie forward, slid off the mare's back, and ran to meet the bedraggled trio. Behind her, she could hear the men following her back to the trail.

"Malinda, how did you do it?" she asked. "How did you get Samuel away from all those Indians?"

Malinda grinned. "We be playing our drum, telling him we were nearby. Samuel pretended to go to the river to get water for the Indians," she explained. "Instead, he slipped into the river, swam across, and followed the drum to us."

"Samuel?" Sarah said, moving over to stand in front of the boy, noting that his black, curly hair had grown long and was studded with burrs. "I'm Sarah, a friend of your pa's," she began. Then, as he looked up at her out of Marcus's soft, dark eyes, she exclaimed, "Oh, you look just like your father!"

A huge, wide grin split the boy's dark face. "Yes, ma'am," he answered shyly, "so I've been told, though I hardly remember my pa."

Sarah noticed that he spoke with a strange awkward tone that she supposed came from so many months of not speaking English.

"Your pa has searched for you and your ma for years, ever since you were taken away from him by the slave trader," she said. "Oh, Samuel, he will be so happy to see you!"

The boy nodded. "I want to see him," he said gravely.

Then, as he and Dulcie were led toward the extra horses Uncle Ethan had brought for them, Sarah noticed that he walked with a limp in his right leg.

"When the Indians first captured him, they broke his leg to keep him from running away," Malinda said beside her. "They made sure it healed crooked to slow him down," she went on. "Then they could leave him free to come and go to wait on them."

Sarah shuddered. "How awful!"

Malinda nodded. "You might say. Though, the Indians' trust in that limp was what gave Samuel the chance to make his escape."

"A blessing in disguise. That's what Ma would likely call it," Sarah muttered, watching her uncle lead a horse toward them that surely had been chosen especially for Malinda. It looked big enough to carry six men!

"The Lord works in mysterious ways," Malinda agreed, taking the reins Uncle Ethan handed her. "Some be calling it magic. Some be calling it old wives' tales," she said, leading the horse over to the bank that rose above the trail. She winked one dark eye at Sarah. "Malinda be calling it miracles," she said with a grin and dropped easily from the bank onto the horse's broad back.

A miracle in itself, Sarah thought, returning the grin.

"Move out!" Uncle Ethan called from the front of the line, and the horses and riders all followed him and the Little Captain down the trail, back the way they had come.

As they rode, Sarah studied Samuel. Marcus had told her so much about his boy, she almost felt she knew him. Of course Sam didn't know her at all, but she knew that as a little boy he had liked helping his pa in the garden. She knew that he had saved the earthworms their hoes uncovered to use for bait when they went fishing in the long summer evenings after chores were done, and that he liked catfish best of all the fish in the James River. She knew that he liked fried chicken, too, and sweet potatoes roasted in the ashes, and warm milk fresh from the cow.

Sarah watched him, riding ahead of her in the saddle Uncle Ethan had placed on the horse. He ignored the reins and guided the animal with the touch of his hand and his knees, just as the Little Captain did. All at once, Sarah remembered Dulcie saying Sam might not want to be rescued. Was he happy to be free of the Indians and on his way home to Williamsburg? Or, in the long months he had spent with them, had he become one of the Indians?

When they made camp for the night, and Sarah had filled

her plate with the biscuits and gravy Malinda had prepared, she went over to sit beside Sam. His mother sat on the other side, reaching out now and then to touch him on the arm, as though she couldn't believe he really was there.

"Are you glad to be going home?" Sarah asked Sam, who was busily sopping up gravy with a biscuit.

He turned to look at her from eyes so like Marcus's they made Sarah homesick for the palace gardens and Marcus's company.

"I want to see my pa," he answered finally, "but I'd rather stay with the Indians than go back to slavery."

"Weren't you a slave to the Indians?" Sarah asked in surprise. "We saw you carrying water to the braves when they besieged the fort."

He sopped up the last of the gravy with the end of his biscuit before he answered. "I had to work for the Indians, yeah. But, ma'am, I started chopping cotton when I was five years old. After they took Ma and me to South Carolina, I was in the fields from sunup to sundown. At least when my chores for the Indians were done, they let me hunt and fish and play games with their young ones. I'd rather stay with the Indians than go back to the slavery of the cotton plantation any time."

Dulcie reached over to pat his arm reassuringly. "They dead!" she whispered.

"That's right," Sarah said. "The people who brought you and Dulcie to Kentucky were all killed by the Indians. You and your ma are free now, Sam. I'm sure Uncle Ethan can get you some kind of legal papers to protect your freedom once you get back to Williamsburg."

His dark eyes studied hers. "I sure hope you're right, ma'am," he said solemnly.

195

"Call me Sarah, Sam," she told him, "and I know I'm right. You and your ma will be free to live with your pa down in Raccoon Trace. He has a nice little house with pretty flowers growing along the brick walk he made. And you can help your pa with the gardens at the Governor's Palace where he works. Did your pa ever take you there? He said you liked to help him in the garden."

Sam shook his head. "Ma and I belonged to a James River plantation. We were not allowed to leave it. Pa always came to visit us," he explained. "We had a small garden out behind our cabin."

"The palace gardens are beautiful, with flowers and geese and swans. I'm sure Marcus will want you to help him tend them," she babbled. "Oh, Sam, he's so nice! You'll enjoy getting to know him again."

He nodded politely, and stood up. "Good night, ma'am," he said.

Sarah sighed. "Good night, Sam," she answered.

"He be a good boy," Dulcie said suddenly to no one in particular, her eyes following Sam to where he had made his bed for the night. "My Samuel, he be a good boy," she repeated, nodding her head.

"And Marcus is a good man, Dulcie," Sarah said, reaching over to pat her on the hand. "You'll be going home to him soon."

Dulcie looked her full in the eyes for the first time since she had met her. "Marcus?" she said softly, as though tasting the name on her tongue. Then a smile started in her dark eyes and spread over her face. "Marcus!" she said, nodding her head. She closed her eyes, and, to Sarah's amazement, she began to sing, a lilting, wordless tune that rose above the trees, rivaling the trills of the wild canary.

★ Chapter Twenty ★

Sarah felt the melody play over her spine. "Marcus was right," she said aloud. "She can sing like a nightingale!"

Sarah saw Uncle Ethan cast a worried glance around the dark circle of trees that surrounded their camp. Then he crossed over to where the Little Captain sat against a tree and bent down to say something in his ear. The Indian got up and disappeared into the forest.

The rest of the men sat as though they had been frozen to the spot, listening to Dulcie's song. Her voice dipped and soared and swirled around them, as though once released, it could not be stopped.

Sarah looked up to see her uncle standing over her. "The woman sings like an angel!" he breathed. Then he cleared his throat. "But I'm afraid she has alerted every Indian in the country to our whereabouts," he said. "Can you get her to stop, Sarah?"

Samuel came over and took his mother protectively by the arm. "I haven't heard her sing like that since they took us away from Pa," he said wonderingly, as he urged her gently away.

Dulcie smiled sweetly at the group, brought the last trill down to an ending, and let Sam lead her to her bed.

Soon afterward, the Little Captain came back into the camp. "No Indian sign anywhere, Colonel Strong Arms," he announced. "Earth tremble with many feet moving north. None traveling south."

Sarah saw her uncle relax. "All right, men," he ordered, "let's get some sleep. I want to be up and on the trail before sunup! Caleb, you take the first watch, and I'll relieve you."

Sarah arose and started toward the bed she had prepared earlier. "Good night, Uncle Ethan," she murmured as she passed him.

"Good night, Sarah," he responded with the old familiar warmth.

Surprised, she looked up and found that he was smiling down at her, his brown eyes kind and loving again. He put an arm around her shoulders and drew her close for a moment.

"I'm so sorry, Uncle Ethan," she whispered brokenly.

"I know you are, dear," he said, "and I accept your apology." Then he shook her a little. "But you will be punished. I . . . "

"I know, Uncle Ethan," she said, laughing shakily as she wiped tears away with her hand. "I don't look forward to it! But you gave your word, and I would be disappointed in you, I reckon, if you didn't keep it."

He laughed with her, hugged her again, and let her go wrap up in her deerskin on the spongy, lumpy cedar boughs that made her bed.

"Whippoorwill! Whippoorwill!" she heard deep in the forest. Instead of Indians, though, tonight the cry made her think of punishment. What would Uncle Ethan demand of her? Whatever it was, she would endure it and then, as Marcus had once told her, put it all behind her and get on with living.

Suddenly Sarah remembered her prayer of the night before. She had told God she wanted Him to direct her paths. She had meant that. Now, she wondered, where would He lead her next? Would she stay at Harrodstown until her family went back to Stoney Creek and then go with them to once again carve a farm out of the wilderness? Would she go back to Williamsburg to learn all she could before she became a teacher? Trying to tutor the Reynolds girls had shown her that she had much yet to learn.

★ Chapter Twenty ★

Like an echo of Dulcie's song, Sarah heard the wind moving through the forest. Was that a wild Kentucky wind calling her name? Or was it a Virginia wind, whispering secrets of home? Her brother Nate had said it was God's voice that called them in the wind and that it reached everywhere. "Someday," he had predicted, "you will hear it calling your name."

Sarah sighed contentedly. It really didn't matter whether she lay in a deep feather bed on a walnut bedstead in Williamsburg, or on a straw mattress supported by ropes in Harrodstown. It didn't matter if she slept in a cabin on Stoney Creek, or out there under the stars on sweet-smelling cedar boughs under a deerskin. She had heard God calling her at last, and she had answered. Sarah's long journey had ended. She was home.

Echoes from the Past

As the Indians saw the white settlers fencing in the meadows and cutting down the forests of their "happy hunting ground," their hatred of these settlers grew. The British were quick to seize this advantage to gain control of Kentucky.

The British military leaders knew that if they could squeeze the colonies between their warships on the eastern coast and the Indians in the western lands, they could soon end the colonists' war for independence. Some said they even offered the Indians money for every settler's scalp. Whether or not that is true, the Indians became merciless in their attacks on the Kentucky settlements.

A visit to the reconstructed forts at Boonesborough and Harrodstown makes it hard to believe that the frail structures could withstand the attacks they received—hundreds of Indian braves pitted against twenty-five riflemen at Boonesborough on a good day, and approximately sixty-five at Harrodstown. Little Saint Asaph (or Logan's Fort) had only fifteen fighting men. But the British and the Indians underestimated the settlers' determination and courage. Somehow, they held on to their tiny settlements in the wilderness.

The names of some of Kentucky's brave pioneers have become a part of history—James Harrod, Benjamin Logan, George Rogers Clark. But, thanks to television, perhaps the best known among them is Daniel Boone, whom modern-day Americans know as a rough frontiersman in a coonskin cap. Boone never wore a coonskin cap, and though he spent much time exploring and enjoying the wilderness, he was not an ignorant backwoodsman. A skilled negotiator, surveyor, and road-builder, he did as much as anyone to open up this new land to settlers. There was a time, though, when old Dan'l was not so widely appreciated in Kentucky.

One day, when Boone and twenty-seven other men were making salt at Blue Licks, they were suddenly surrounded by about two hundred Shawnee Indians. After negotiating with the Indians, Boone persuaded his companions to surrender, believing this was the only way to save their lives since the Indians promised they would not harm them. The Indians kept their promise and soon released their prisoners to the British, unharmed. They didn't release Boone, however, whom they took with them back to their village in the Ohio territory. There he was adopted by Chief Blackfish and given the Indian name of "Big Turtle." He was allowed to roam the nearby forest, fishing and hunting.

Then, Boone overheard the Indians plotting an attack on the fort that was named for him—Boonesborough. He escaped and headed for the fort, traveling 160 miles on foot in ten days, stopping only once to prepare and eat a meal. Realizing Boone had gone to warn the settlers, the Indians postponed their attack for several weeks.

Some of the settlers, though, became suspicious of Boone's ability to come and go among the Indians so freely. He obviously had great respect for them, spoke their languages, and claimed to have killed only one Indian in his life. Eventually, he was brought to trial for treason. Evidence of Boone's heroic deeds on behalf of the settlements, however, convinced the jury he was innocent.

Kentucky's pioneer women fought right along with the men. Countless stories of their bravery have come down through the years. One such story, which has a humorous twist, tells of a woman at Fort Harrod who borrowed her neighbor's hat. She wore it one morning when she and some of the other women of the fort—accompanied by a few of the men—went to milk the cows that had been left to forage for food at the edge of the forest. When the small party was attacked by Indians and fled for their lives toward the fort, the woman's borrowed hat flew off her head. She stopped, ran back toward the pursuing braves, snatched the hat from the ground, and ran with it to safety inside the stockade. Good hats were hard to come by in the wilderness, and apparently, she respected the rights of the woman who owned the hat more than she feared the Indians!

This same determination and courage has led Kentuckians, from pioneer days to the present, to be among the first to volunteer to fight our country's battles. Throughout our nation's history, Kentucky has provided more than its share of soldiers for any war. During the

★ Reunion in Kentucky ★

Revolutionary War, as though they didn't have enough to do with fighting the Indians, the Kentucky pioneers volunteered to go to Tennessee to fight the British in the Battle of Kings Mountain—and provided their own clothing, guns, and supplies. And true to the independent pioneer spirit, when Americans fought each other in the great Civil War, almost as many Kentuckians wore Confederate gray as Yankee blue.

What happened to the families that George Rogers Clark left on Corn Island? They soon crossed to the south side of the Ohio River and began a settlement that grew to be the city of Louisville, Kentucky's largest city. It was named for King Louis XVI of France because of his decision to assist the American colonists in their war for independence. The north side of the river there eventually became the state of Indiana.

Slaves were brought to Kentucky by their owners to help clear land and tend crops. Two years after Sarah discovered Malinda at Fort Harrod, the count of Kentuckians included 61,133 white settlers, 12,430 slaves, and 114 free African Americans. African Americans contributed much to the settlement of this new land, some of them becoming skilled stone masons, blacksmiths, shoemakers, and other craftsmen.

Though there were some in Kentucky who gave God little thought except to take His name in vain, faith in God was very important to most of the pioneers. A clergyman from the Church of England held the first religious service in Kentucky under the shade of a huge elm tree at Boonesborough in May of 1775. A year later, about the time Sarah and her family moved to Kentucky, two Baptist ministers held services under the limbs of a great elm at the big spring at Harrodstown. These pioneer preachers were soon followed by the Presbyterians, the Methodists, and the Catholics.

The first school in Kentucky was the poor little log one Sarah visited at Harrodstown, and it was followed by one at Boonesborough three years later. In Sarah's day, girls did not attend school, but Kentucky girls have been allowed to go to school since the early 1800's.

Just as Sarah's pa predicted, beautiful homes, churches, and government buildings have replaced the crude log structures of early Kentucky. Industry and business opportunities continue to grow. Modern schools and universities abound.

Kentucky is still a "land of tomorrow," as the Indians sometimes called it, but its people have not forgotten their past. The rebuilt forts and many other historical monuments and museums allow visitors a glimpse into those days when the survival of the new settlements depended upon the sacrifices and determination of a handful of brave pioneers. Without them, there would be no Commonwealth of Kentucky.

Where did Sarah Moore fit into all of this development? Did she go back to Williamsburg to study? Did she return to Stoney Creek to help her family rebuild their home there? Or did she, in turn, do both? What do you think? You are probably right.

Home on Stoney Creek

"Kentucky! Why do we have to move to Kentucky?"

The cry for freedom is spreading throughout the colonies calling many people to war, but not Sarah's family. The cry they hear leads them to a new, untamed wilderness called Kentucky.

Sleeping on pine boughs covered with deerskins, having no one her age to talk to, fighting off pig-eating bears—Kentucky doesn't feel much like freedom to Sarah. She can't understand why God didn't answer her prayers to stay in Virginia, but she vows she'll return some day.

Wanda Luttrell was raised and still lives on the banks of Stoney Creek. Wanda and her husband have shared their home on Stoney Creek with their five children.

Be sure to read all the books in Sarah's Journey:

Home on Stoney Creek
Stranger in Williamsburg
Reunion in Kentucky

Also available as an audio book:
Home on Stoney Creek

Stranger in Williamsburg

"A spy? Gabrielle can't be a spy!"

The American Revolution is in full swing, and Sarah Moore is caught right in the middle of it. When she returned to Virginia to live with her aunt's family and learn from their tutor, she certainly had no plans to get involved with a possible spy.

With a war going on, her family back in Kentucky, and people choosing sides all around her, Sarah has begun to wonder if she can trust anyone—even God.

Wanda Luttrell was raised and still lives on the banks of Stoney Creek, Sarah's Kentucky home. Wanda and her husband have shared their home on Stoney Creek with their five children.

Be sure to read all the books in Sarah's Journey:

Home on Stoney Creek
Stranger in Williamsburg
Reunion in Kentucky

Also available as an audio book:
Home on Stoney Creek

Grandma's Attic Series

Pieces of Magic

Remember when you were a child—when all the world was new, and the smallest object a thing of wonder? Arleta Richardson remembers: the funny wearable wire contraption hidden in the dusty attic, the century-old schoolchild's slate which belonged to Grandma, an ancient trunk filled with quilt pieces—each with its own special story—and the button basket, a miracle of mysteries. And best of all was the remarkable grandmother who made magic of all she touched, bringing the past alive as only a born storyteller could.

Here are those marvelous tales—faithfully recalled for the delight of young and old alike, a touchstone to another day when life was simpler, perhaps richer; when the treasures of family life and love were passed from generation to generation by a child's questions . . . and the legends that followed enlarged our faith.

Arleta Richardson has written the beloved Grandma's Attic series as well as the Orphans' Journey series. She lives in California where she continues writing and public speaking.

Be sure to read all the books from
Grandma's Attic:

In Grandma's Attic
More Stories from Grandma's Attic
Still More Stories from Grandma's Attic
Treasure from Grandma

The Grandma's Attic Novels

At home in North Branch—what could be better?

The Grandma's Attic Novels bring you the story of Mabel O'Dell's young adult years as she becomes a teacher, wife, and mother. Join Mabel and her best friend, Sarah Jane, as they live, laugh, and learn together. They rise to each occasion they meet with their usual measure of hilarity, anguish, and newfound insights, all the while learning more of what it means to live a life of faith.

Arleta Richardson has written the beloved Grandma's Attic series as well as the Orphans' Journey series. She lives in California where she continues writing and public speaking.

Be sure to read all the Grandma's Attic novels:

Away from Home
A School of Her Own
Wedding Bells Ahead
At Home in North Branch
New Faces, New Friends
Stories from the Growing Years

❧ PARENTS ❧

Are you looking for fun ways to bring the Bible to life in the lives of your children?

Chariot Family Publishing has hundreds of books, toys, games, and videos that help teach your children the Bible and apply it to their everyday lives.

Look for these educational, inspirational, and fun products at your local Christian bookstore.

DATE DUE

₹ 32	MAY 0 4 1999	
	MAY 0 6 1999	
	FEB 2 2 2000	
MAR 0 3 2000		
JAN 1 9 2001 JAN 2 6 2001		